EAST, WEST

SALMAN RUSHDIE

EAST, WEST

STORIES

PANTHEON BOOKS   NEW YORK

LIBRARY OF CONGRESS CATALOGING-IN-PUBLICATION DATA
Rushdie, Salman
East, West: stories /Salman Rushdie
p.   cm.
ISBN: 0-679-43965-X
I. Title.
PR6068.U757E27   1995
823' .914—DC20   94-28277

Manufactured in the United States of America

First American Edition

2   4   6   8   9   7   5   3   1

for Andrew and Gillon

CONTENTS

EAST

GOOD ADVICE IS
RARER THAN RUBIES

On the last Tuesday of the month, the dawn bus, its headlamps still shining, brought Miss Rehana to the gates of the British Consulate. It arrived pushing a cloud of dust, veiling her beauty from the eyes of strangers until she descended. The bus was brightly painted in multicoloured arabesques, and on the front it said 'MOVE OVER DARLING' in green and gold letters; on the back it added 'TATA-BATA' and also 'O.K. GOOD-LIFE'. Miss Rehana told the driver it was a beautiful bus, and he jumped down and held the door open for her, bowing theatrically as she descended.

Miss Rehana's eyes were large and black and bright enough not to need the help of antimony, and when the advice expert Muhammad Ali saw them he felt himself becoming young again. He watched her approaching the Consulate gates as the light strengthened, and asking the bearded lala who guarded them in a gold-buttoned khaki uniform with a cockaded turban when they would open. The lala, usually so rude to the Consulate's Tuesday women, answered Miss Rehana with something like courtesy.

'Half an hour,' he said gruffly. 'Maybe two hours. Who knows? The sahibs are eating their breakfast.'

The dusty compound between the bus stop and the Consulate was already full of Tuesday women, some veiled, a few barefaced like Miss Rehana. They all looked frightened, and leaned heavily on the arms of uncles or brothers, who were trying to look confident. But Miss Rehana had come on her own, and did not seem at all alarmed.

Muhammad Ali, who specialised in advising the most vulnerable-looking of these weekly supplicants, found his feet leading him towards the strange, big-eyed, independent girl.

'Miss,' he began. 'You have come for permit to London, I think so?'

She was standing at a hot-snack stall in the little shanty-town by the edge of the compound, munching chilli-pakoras contentedly. She turned to look at him, and at close range those eyes did bad things to his digestive tract.

'Yes, I have.'

'Then, please, you allow me to give some advice? Small cost only.'

Miss Rehana smiled. 'Good advice is rarer than rubies,' she said. 'But alas, I cannot pay. I am an orphan, not one of your wealthy ladies.'

'Trust my grey hairs,' Muhammad Ali urged her.

'My advice is well tempered by experience. You will certainly find it good.'

She shook her head. 'I tell you I am a poor potato. There are women here with male family members, all earning good wages. Go to them. Good advice should find good money.'

I am going crazy, Muhammad Ali thought, because he heard his voice telling her of its own volition, 'Miss, I have been drawn to you by Fate. What to do? Our meeting was written. I also am a poor man only, but for you my advice comes free.'

She smiled again. 'Then I must surely listen. When Fate sends a gift, one receives good fortune.'

He led her to the low wooden desk in his own special corner of the shanty-town. She followed, continuing to eat pakoras from a little newspaper packet. She did not offer him any.

Muhammad Ali put a cushion on the dusty ground. 'Please to sit.' She did as he asked. He sat cross-legged across the desk from her, conscious that two or three dozen pairs of male eyes were watching him enviously, that all the other shanty-town men were ogling the latest young lovely to be charmed by the old grey-hair fraud. He took a deep breath to settle himself.

'Name, please.'

'Miss Rehana,' she told him. 'Fiancée of Mustafa Dar of Bradford, London.'

'Bradford, England,' he corrected her gently. 'London is a town only, like Multan or Bahawalpur. England is a great nation full of the coldest fish in the world.'

'I see. Thank you,' she responded gravely, so that he was unsure if she was making fun of him.

'You have filled application form? Then let me see, please.'

She passed him a neatly folded document in a brown envelope.

'Is it OK?' For the first time there was a note of anxiety in her voice.

He patted the desk quite near the place where her hand rested. 'I am certain,' he said. 'Wait on and I will check.'

She finished the pakoras while he scanned her papers.

'Tip-top,' he pronounced at length. 'All in order.'

'Thank you for your advice,' she said, making as if to rise. 'I'll go now and wait by the gate.'

'What are you thinking?' he cried loudly, smiting his forehead. 'You consider this is easy business? Just give the form and poof, with a big smile they hand over the permit? Miss Rehana, I tell you, you are entering a worse place than any police station.'

'Is it so, truly?' His oratory had done the trick. She was a captive audience now, and he would be able to look at her for a few moments longer.

Drawing another calming breath, he launched into his set speech. He told her that the sahibs thought that all the women who came on Tuesdays, claiming to be dependents of bus drivers in Luton or chartered accountants in Manchester, were crooks and liars and cheats.

She protested, 'But then I will simply tell them that I, for one, am no such thing!'

Her innocence made him shiver with fear for her. She was a sparrow, he told her, and they were men with hooded eyes, like hawks. He explained that they would ask her questions, personal questions, questions such as a lady's own brother would be too shy to ask. They would ask if she was virgin, and, if not, what her fiancé's love-making habits were, and what secret nicknames they had invented for one another.

Muhammad Ali spoke brutally, on purpose, to lessen the shock she would feel when it, or something like it, actually happened. Her eyes remained steady, but her hands began to flutter at the edges of the desk.

He went on:

'They will ask you how many rooms are in your

family home, and what colour are the walls, and what days do you empty the rubbish. They will ask your man's mother's third cousin's aunt's step-daughter's middle name. And all these things they have already asked your Mustafa Dar in his Bradford. And if you make one mistake, you are finished.'

'Yes,' she said, and he could hear her disciplining her voice. 'And what is your advice, old man?'

It was at this point that Muhammad Ali usually began to whisper urgently, to mention that he knew a man, a very good type, who worked in the Consulate, and through him, for a fee, the necessary papers could be delivered, with all the proper authenticating seals. Business was good, because the women would often pay him five hundred rupees or give him a gold bracelet for his pains, and go away happy.

They came from hundreds of miles away – he normally made sure of this before beginning to trick them – so even when they discovered they had been swindled they were unlikely to return. They went away to Sargodha or Lalukhet and began to pack, and who knows at what point they found out they had been gulled, but it was at a too-late point, anyway.

Life is hard, and an old man must live by his wits. It

was not up to Muhammad Ali to have compassion for these Tuesday women.

But once again his voice betrayed him, and instead of starting his customary speech it began to reveal to her his greatest secret.

'Miss Rehana,' his voice said, and he listened to it in amazement, 'you are a rare person, a jewel, and for you I will do what I would not do for my own daughter, perhaps. One document has come into my possession that can solve all your worries at one stroke.'

'And what is this sorcerer's paper?' she asked, her eyes unquestionably laughing at him now.

His voice fell low-as-low.

'Miss Rehana, it is a British passport. Completely genuine and pukka goods. I have a good friend who will put your name and photo, and then, hey-presto, England there you come!'

He had said it!

Anything was possible now, on this day of his insanity. Probably he would give her the thing free-gratis, and then kick himself for a year afterwards.

Old fool, he berated himself. *The oldest fools are bewitched by the youngest girls.*

———

'Let me understand you,' she was saying. 'You are proposing I should commit a crime . . .'

'Not crime,' he interposed. 'Facilitation.'

' . . . and go to Bradford, London, illegally, and therefore justify the low opinion the Consulate sahibs have of us all. Old babuji, this is not good advice.'

'Bradford, *England*,' he corrected her mournfully. 'You should not take my gift in such a spirit.'

'Then how?'

'Bibi, I am a poor fellow, and I have offered this prize because you are so beautiful. Do not spit on my generosity. Take the thing. Or else don't take, go home, forget England, only do not go into that building and lose your dignity.'

But she was on her feet, turning away from him, walking towards the gates, where the women had begun to cluster and the lala was swearing at them to be patient or none of them would be admitted at all.

'So be a fool,' Muhammad Ali shouted after her. 'What goes of my father's if you are?' (Meaning, what was it to him.)

She did not turn.

'It is the curse of our people,' he yelled. 'We are poor, we are ignorant, and we completely refuse to learn.'

'Hey, Muhammad Ali,' the woman at the betel-nut

stall called across to him. 'Too bad, she likes them young.'

That day Muhammad Ali did nothing but stand around near the Consulate gates. Many times he scolded himself, *Go from here, old goof, lady does not desire to speak with you any further.* But when she came out, she found him waiting.

'Salaam, advice wallah,' she greeted him.

She seemed calm, and at peace with him again, and he thought, *My God, ya Allah, she has pulled it off. The British sahibs also have been drowning in her eyes and she has got her passage to England.*

He smiled at her hopefully. She smiled back with no trouble at all.

'Miss Rehana Begum,' he said, 'felicitations, daughter, on what is obviously your hour of triumph.'

Impulsively, she took his forearm in her hand.

'Come,' she said. 'Let me buy you a pakora to thank you for your advice and to apologise for my rudeness, too.'

They stood in the dust of the afternoon compound near the bus, which was getting ready to leave. Coolies were tying bedding rolls to the roof. A hawker shouted at the passengers, trying to sell them love stories and green medicines, both of which cured unhappiness. Miss Rehana and a happy Muhammad Ali ate their pakoras sitting on the bus's 'front mud-guard', that is, the bumper. The old advice expert began softly to hum a tune from a movie soundtrack. The day's heat was gone.

'It was an arranged engagement,' Miss Rehana said all at once. 'I was nine years old when my parents fixed it. Mustafa Dar was already thirty at that time, but my father wanted someone who could look after me as he had done himself and Mustafa was a man known to Daddyji as a solid type. Then my parents died and Mustafa Dar went to England and said he would send for me. That was many years ago. I have his photo, but he is like a stranger to me. Even his voice, I do not recognise it on the phone.'

The confession took Muhammad Ali by surprise, but he nodded with what he hoped looked like wisdom.

'Still and after all,' he said, 'one's parents act in one's best interests. They found you a good and honest man who has kept his word and sent for you. And now you have a lifetime to get to know him, and to love.'

———

He was puzzled, now, by the bitterness that had infected her smile.

'But, old man,' she asked him, 'why have you already packed me and posted me off to England?'

He stood up, shocked.

'You looked happy – so I just assumed . . . excuse me, but they turned you down or what?'

'I got all their questions wrong,' she replied. 'Distinguishing marks I put on the wrong cheeks, bathroom decor I completely redecorated, all absolutely topsy-turvy, you see.'

'But what to do? How will you go?'

'Now I will go back to Lahore and my job. I work in a great house, as ayah to three good boys. They would have been sad to see me leave.'

'But this is tragedy!' Muhammad Ali lamented. 'Oh, how I pray that you had taken up my offer! Now, but, it is not possible, I regret to inform. Now they have your form on file, cross-check can be made, even the passport will not suffice.

'It is spoilt, all spoilt, and it could have been so easy if advice had been accepted in good time.'

'I do not think,' she told him, 'I truly do not think you should be sad.'

Her last smile, which he watched from the compound until the bus concealed it in a dust-cloud, was the happiest thing he had ever seen in his long, hot, hard, unloving life.

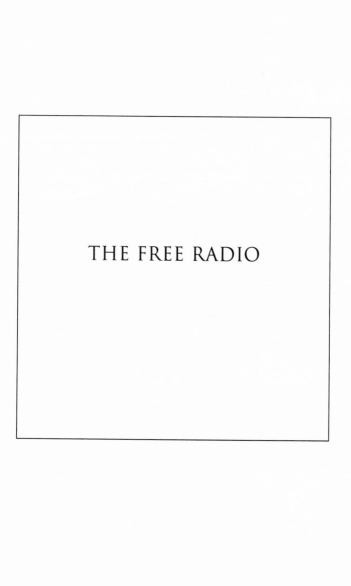

THE FREE RADIO

We all knew nothing good would happen to him while the thief's widow had her claws dug into his flesh, but the boy was an innocent, a real donkey's child, you can't teach such people.

That boy could have had a good life. God had blessed him with God's own looks, and his father had gone to the grave for him, but didn't he leave the boy a brand-new first-class cycle rickshaw with plastic covered seats and all? So: looks he had, his own trade he had, there would have been a good wife in time, he should just have taken out some years to save some rupees; but no, he must fall for a thief's widow before the hairs had time to come out on his chin, before his milk-teeth had split, one might say.

We felt bad for him, but who listens to the wisdom of the old today?

I say: who listens?

Exactly; nobody, certainly not a stone-head like Ramani the rickshaw-wallah. But I blame the widow. I saw it happen, you know, I saw most of it until I couldn't stand any more. I sat under this very banyan, smoking this selfsame hookah, and not much escaped my notice.

And at one time I tried to save him from his fate, but it was no go . . .

The widow was certainly attractive, no point denying, in a sort of hard vicious way she was all right, but it is her mentality that was rotten. Ten years older than Ramani she must have been, five children alive and two dead, what that thief did besides robbing and making babies God only knows, but he left her not one new paisa, so of course she would be interested in Ramani. I'm not saying a rickshaw-wallah makes much in this town but two mouthfuls are better to eat than wind. And not many people will look twice at the widow of a good-for-nothing.

They met right here.

One day Ramani rode into town without a passenger, but grinning as usual as if someone had given him a ten-chip tip, singing some playback music from the radio, his hair greased like for a wedding. He was not such a fool that he didn't know how the girls watched him all the time and passed remarks about his long and well-muscled legs.

The thief's widow had gone to the bania shop to buy some three grains of dal and I won't say where the money came from, but people saw men at night near her rutputty shack, even the bania himself they were telling me but I personally will not comment.

She had all her five brats with her and then and there,

cool as a fan, she called out: '*Hey! Rickshaaa!*' Loud, you know, like a truly cheap type. Showing us she can afford to ride in rickshaws, as if anyone was interested. Her children must have gone hungry to pay for the ride but in my opinion it was an investment for her, because must-be she had decided already to put her hooks into Ramani. So they all poured into the rickshaw and he took her away, and with the five kiddies as well as the widow there was quite a weight, so he was puffing hard, and the veins were standing out on his legs, and I thought, careful, my son, or you will have this burden to pull for all of your life.

But after that Ramani and the thief's widow were seen everywhere, shamelessly, in public places, and I was glad his mother was dead because if she had lived to see this her face would have fallen off from shame.

Sometimes in those days Ramani came into this street in the evenings to meet some friends, and they thought they were very smart because they would go into the back room of the Irani's canteen and drink illegal liquor, only of course everybody knew, but who would do anything, if boys ruin their lives let their relations worry.

I was sad to see Ramani fall into this bad company. His parents were known to me when alive. But when I told Ramani to keep away from those hot-shots he grinned like a sheep and said I was wrong, nothing bad was taking place.

Let it go, I thought.

I knew those cronies of his. They all wore the arm-bands of the new Youth Movement. This was the time of the State of Emergency, and these friends were not peaceful persons, there were stories of beatings-up, so I sat quiet under my tree. Ramani wore no armband but he went with them because they impressed him, the fool.

These armband youths were always flattering Ramani. Such a handsome chap, they told him, compared to you Shashi Kapoor and Amitabh are like lepers only, you should go to Bombay and be put in the motion pictures.

They flattered him with dreams because they knew they could take money from him at cards and he would buy them drink while they did it, though he was no richer than they. So now Ramani's head became filled with these movie dreams, because there was nothing else inside to take up any space, and this is another reason why I blame the widow woman, because she had more years and should have had more sense. In two ticks she could have made him forget all about it, but no, I heard her telling him one day for all to hear, 'Truly you have the looks of Lord Krishna himself, except you are not blue all over.' In the street! So all would know they were lovers! From that day on I was sure a disaster would happen.

The next time the thief's widow came into the street to visit the bania shop I decided to act. Not for my own sake but for the boy's dead parents I risked being shamed by a . . . no, I will not call her the name, she is elsewhere now and they will know what she is like.

'Thief's widow!' I called out.

She stopped dead, jerking her face in an ugly way, as if I had hit her with a whip.

'Come here and speak,' I told her.

Now she could not refuse because I am not without importance in the town and maybe she calculated that if people saw us talking they would stop ignoring her when she passed, so she came as I knew she would.

'I have to say this thing only,' I told her with dignity. 'Ramani the rickshaw boy is dear to me, and you must find some person of your own age, or, better still, go to the widows' ashrams in Benares and spend the rest of your life there in holy prayer, thanking God that widow-burning is now illegal.'

So at this point she tried to shame me by screaming

out and calling me curses and saying that I was a poisonous old man who should have died years ago, and then she said, 'Let me tell you, mister teacher sahib *retired*, that your Ramani has asked to marry me and I have said no, because I wish no more children, and he is a young man and should have his own. So tell that to the whole world and stop your cobra poison.'

For a time after that I closed my eyes to this affair of Ramani and the thief's widow, because I had done all I could and there were many other things in the town to interest a person like myself. For instance, the local health officer had brought a big white caravan into the street and was given permission to park it out of the way under the banyan tree; and every night men were taken into this van for a while and things were done to them.

I did not care to be in the vicinity at these times, because the youths with armbands were always in attendance, so I took my hookah and sat in another place. I heard rumours of what was happening in the caravan but I closed my ears.

But it was while this caravan, which smelled of ether, was in town that the extent of the widow's wickedness became plain; because at this time Ramani suddenly began to talk about his new fantasy, telling everyone he could find that very shortly he was to receive a highly special and personalised gift from the Central Government in Delhi itself, and this gift was to be a brand-new first-class battery-operated transistor radio.

Now then: we had always believed that our Ramani was a little soft in the head, with his notions of being a film star and what all; so most of us just nodded tolerantly and said, 'Yes, Ram, that is nice for you,' and, 'What a fine, generous Government it is that gives radios to persons who are so keen on popular music.'

But Ramani insisted it was true, and seemed happier than at any time in his life, a happiness which could not be explained simply by the supposed imminence of the transistor.

Soon after the dream-radio was first mentioned, Ramani and the thief's widow were married, and then I understood everything. I did not attend the nuptials – it was a poor affair by all accounts – but not long afterwards I spoke to Ram when he came past the banyan with an empty rickshaw one day.

He came to sit by me and I asked, 'My child, did you go to the caravan? What have you let them do to you?'

'Don't worry,' he replied. 'Everything is tremendously wonderful. I am in love, teacher sahib, and I have made it possible for me to marry my woman.'

I confess I became angry; indeed, I almost wept as I realised that Ramani had gone voluntarily to subject himself to a humiliation which was being forced upon the other men who were taken to the caravan. I reproved him bitterly. 'My idiot child, you have let that woman deprive you of your manhood!'

'It is not so bad,' Ram said, meaning the *nasbandi*. 'It does not stop love-making or anything, excuse me, teacher sahib, for speaking of such a thing. It stops babies only and my woman did not want children any more, so now all is hundred per cent OK. Also it is in national interest,' he pointed out. 'And soon the free radio will arrive.'

'The free radio,' I repeated.

'Yes, remember, teacher sahib,' Ram said confidentially, 'some years back, in my kiddie days, when Laxman the tailor had this operation? In no time the radio came and from all over town people gathered to listen to it. It is how the Government says thank you. It will be excellent to have.'

'Go away, get away from me,' I cried out in despair, and did not have the heart to tell him what everyone else in the country already knew, which was that the free radio scheme was a dead duck, long gone, long forgotten. It had been over – *funtoosh!* – for years.

———

After these events the thief's widow, who was now Ram's wife, did not come into town very often, no doubt being too ashamed of what she had made him do, but Ramani worked longer hours than ever before, and every time he saw any of the dozens of people he'd told about the radio he would put one hand up to his ear as if he were already holding the blasted machine in it, and he would mimic broadcasts with a certain energetic skill.

'*Yé Akashvani hai*,' he announced to the streets. 'This is All-India Radio. Here is the news. A Government spokesman today announced that Ramani rickshaw-wallah's radio was on its way and would be delivered at any moment. And now some playback music.' After which he would sing songs by Asha Bhonsle or Lata Mangeshkar in a high, ridiculous falsetto.

Ram always had the rare quality of total belief in his dreams, and there were times when his faith in the imaginary radio almost took us in, so that we half-believed it was really on its way, or even that it was already there, cupped invisibly against his ear as he rode his rickshaw around the streets of the town. We began to expect to hear Ramani, around a corner or at the far end of a lane, ringing his bell and yelling cheerfully:

'All-India Radio! This is All-India Radio!'

———

Time passed. Ram continued to carry the invisible radio around town. One year passed. Still his caricatures of the radio channel filled the air in the streets. But when I saw him now, there was a new thing in his face, a strained thing, as if he were having to make a phenomenal effort, which was much more tiring than driving a rickshaw, more tiring even than pulling a rickshaw containing a thief's widow and her five living children and the ghosts of two dead ones; as if all the energy of his young body was being poured into that fictional space between his ear and his hand, and he was trying to bring the radio into existence by a mighty, and possibly fatal, act of will.

I felt most helpless, I can tell you, because I had divined that Ram had poured into the idea of the radio all his worries and regrets about what he had done, and that if the dream were to die he would be forced to face the full gravity of his crime against his own body, to understand that the thief's widow had turned him, before she married him, into a thief of a stupid and terrible kind, because she had made him rob himself.

And then the white caravan came back to its place under the banyan tree and I knew there was nothing to be done, because Ram would certainly come to get his gift.

———

He did not come for one day, then for two, and I learned afterwards that he had not wished to seem greedy; he didn't want the health officer to think he was desperate for the radio. Besides, he was half hoping they would come over and give it to him at his place, perhaps with some kind of small, formal presentation ceremony. A fool is a fool and there is no accounting for his notions.

On the third day he came. Ringing his bicycle-bell and imitating weather forecasts, ear cupped as usual, he arrived at the caravan. And in the rickshaw behind him sat the thief's widow, the witch, who had not been able to resist coming along to watch her companion's destruction.

It did not take very long.

Ram went into the caravan gaily, waving at his arm-banded cronies who were guarding it against the anger of the people, and I am told – for I had left the scene to spare myself the pain – that his hair was well-oiled and his clothes were freshly starched. The thief's widow did not move from the rickshaw, but sat there with a black sari pulled over her head, clutching at her children as if they were straws.

After a short time there were sounds of disagreement inside the caravan, and then louder noises still, and finally the youths in armbands went in to see what was becoming, and soon after that Ram was frogmarched out by his drinking-chums, and his hair-grease was smudged on to his face and there was blood coming from his mouth. His hand was no longer cupped by his ear.

And still – they tell me – the thief's black widow did not move from her place in the rickshaw, although they dumped her husband in the dust.

Yes, I know, I'm an old man, my ideas are wrinkled with age, and these days they tell me sterilisation and God knows what is necessary, and maybe I'm wrong to blame the widow as well – why not? Maybe all the views of the old can be discounted now, and if that's so, let it be. But I'm telling this story and I haven't finished yet.

Some days after the incident at the caravan I saw Ramani selling his rickshaw to the old Muslim crook who runs the bicycle-repair shop. When he saw me watching, Ram came to me and said, 'Goodbye, teacher sahib, I am off to Bombay, where I will become a bigger film star than Shashi Kapoor or Amitabh Bachchan even.'

' "*I* am off," you say?' I asked him. 'Are you perhaps travelling alone?'

He stiffened. The thief's widow had already taught him not to be humble in the presence of elders.

'My wife and children will come also,' he said. It was the last time we spoke. They left that same day on the down train.

After some months had passed I got his first letter, which was not written by himself, of course, since in spite of all my long-ago efforts he barely knew how to write. He had paid a professional letter-writer, which must have cost him many rupees, because everything in life costs money and in Bombay it costs twice as much. Don't ask me why he wrote to me, but he did. I have the letters and can give you proof positive, so maybe there are some uses for old people still, or maybe he knew I was the only one who would be interested in his news.

Anyhow: the letters were full of his new career, they told me how he'd been discovered at once, a big studio had given him a test, now they were grooming him for stardom, he spent his days at the Sun'n'Sand Hotel at Juhu beach in the company of top lady artistes, he was buying a big house at Pali Hill, built in the split-level mode and incorporating the latest security equipment to protect him from the movie fans, the thief's widow was well and happy and getting fat, and life was filled with light and success and no-questions-asked alcohol.

They were wonderful letters, brimming with confidence, but whenever I read them, and sometimes I read them still, I remember the expression which came over his face in the days just before he learned the truth about his radio, and the huge mad energy which he had poured into the act of conjuring reality, by an act of magnificent faith, out of the hot thin air between his cupped hand and his ear.

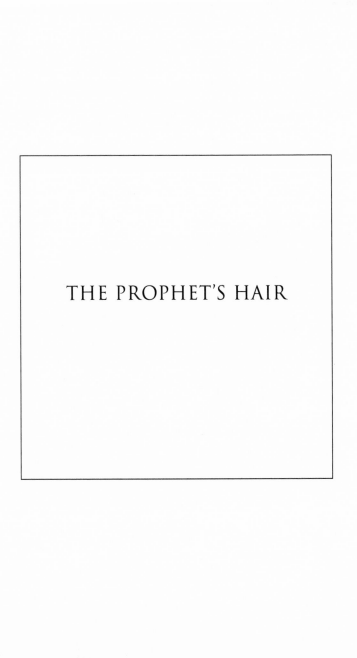

THE PROPHET'S HAIR

Early in the year 19—, when Srinagar was under the spell of a winter so fierce it could crack men's bones as if they were glass, a young man upon whose cold-pinked skin there lay, like a frost, the unmistakable sheen of wealth was to be seen entering the most wretched and disreputable part of the city, where the houses of wood and corrugated iron seemed perpetually on the verge of losing their balance, and asking in low, grave tones where he might go to engage the services of a dependably professional burglar. The young man's name was Atta, and the rogues in that part of town directed him gleefully into ever darker and less public alleys, until in a yard wet with the blood of a slaughtered chicken he was set upon by two men whose faces he never saw, robbed of the substantial bank-roll which he had insanely brought on his solitary excursion, and beaten within an inch of his life.

Night fell. His body was carried by anonymous hands to the edge of the lake, whence it was transported by shikara across the water and deposited, torn and bleeding, on the deserted embankment of the canal which led to the gardens of Shalimar. At dawn the next morning a flower-vendor was rowing his boat through water to which the cold of the night had given the cloudy consistency of wild honey when he saw the

prone form of young Atta, who was just beginning to
stir and moan, and on whose now deathly pale skin the
sheen of wealth could still be made out dimly beneath
an actual layer of frost.

The flower-vendor moored his craft and by stooping
over the mouth of the injured man was able to learn the
poor fellow's address, which was mumbled through lips
that could scarcely move; whereupon, hoping for a
large tip, the hawker rowed Atta home to a large house
on the shores of the lake, where a beautiful but inexplic-
ably bruised young woman and her distraught, but
equally handsome mother, neither of whom, it was
clear from their eyes, had slept a wink from worrying,
screamed at the sight of their Atta – who was the
elder brother of the beautiful young woman – lying
motionless amidst the funereally stunted winter blooms
of the hopeful florist.

The flower-vendor was indeed paid off handsomely,
not least to ensure his silence, and plays no further
part in our story. Atta himself, suffering terribly from
exposure as well as a broken skull, entered a coma
which caused the city's finest doctors to shrug help-
lessly. It was therefore all the more remarkable that on
the very next evening the most wretched and disreputable part of the city received a second unexpected

visitor. This was Huma, the sister of the unfortunate young man, and her question was the same as her brother's, and asked in the same low, grave tones:

'Where may I hire a thief?'

The story of the rich idiot who had come looking for a burglar was already common knowledge in those insalubrious gullies, but this time the young woman added: 'I should say that I am carrying no money, nor am I wearing any jewellery items. My father has disowned me and will pay no ransom if I am kidnapped; and a letter has been lodged with the Deputy Commissioner of Police, my uncle, to be opened in the event of my not being safe at home by morning. In that letter he will find full details of my journey here, and he will move Heaven and Earth to punish my assailants.'

Her exceptional beauty, which was visible even through the enormous welts and bruises disfiguring her arms and forehead, coupled with the oddity of her inquiries, had attracted a sizable group of curious onlookers, and because her little speech seemed to them to cover just about everything, no one attempted to injure her in any way, although there were some raucous comments to the effect that it was pretty peculiar for someone who was trying to hire a crook to invoke the protection of a high-up policeman uncle.

She was directed into ever darker and less public alleys until finally in a gully as dark as ink an old woman with eyes which stared so piercingly that Huma instantly understood she was blind motioned her through a doorway from which darkness seemed to be pouring like smoke. Clenching her fists, angrily ordering her heart to behave normally, Huma followed the old woman into the gloom-wrapped house.

The faintest conceivable rivulet of candlelight trickled through the darkness; following this unreliable yellow thread (because she could no longer see the old lady), Huma received a sudden sharp blow to the shins and cried out involuntarily, after which she at once bit her lip, angry at having revealed her mounting terror to whoever or whatever waited before her, shrouded in blackness.

She had, in fact, collided with a low table on which a single candle burned and beyond which a mountainous figure could be made out, sitting cross-legged on the floor. 'Sit, sit,' said a man's calm, deep voice, and her legs, needing no more flowery invitation, buckled beneath her at the terse command. Clutching her left hand in her right, she forced her voice to respond evenly:

'And you, sir, will be the thief I have been requesting?'

Shifting its weight very slightly, the shadow-mountain informed Huma that all criminal activity originating in this zone was well organised and also centrally controlled, so that all requests for what might be termed freelance work had to be channelled through this room.

He demanded comprehensive details of the crime to be committed, including a precise inventory of items to be acquired, also a clear statement of all financial inducements being offered with no gratuities excluded, plus, for filing purposes only, a summary of the motives for the application.

At this, Huma, as though remembering something, stiffened both in body and resolve and replied loudly that her motives were entirely a matter for herself; that she would discuss details with no one but the thief himself; but that the rewards she proposed could only be described as 'lavish'.

'All I am willing to disclose to you, sir, since it appears that I am on the premises of some sort of employment agency, is that in return for such lavish rewards I must have the most desperate criminal at your disposal, a man for whom life holds no terrors, not even the fear of God.

'The worst of fellows, I tell you – nothing less will do!'

At this a paraffin storm-lantern was lighted, and Huma saw facing her a grey-haired giant down whose left cheek ran the most sinister of scars, a cicatrice in the shape of the letter *sín* in the Nastaliq script. She was gripped by the insupportably nostalgic notion that the bogeyman of her childhood nursery had risen up to confront her, because her ayah had always forestalled any incipient acts of disobedience by threatening Huma and Atta: 'You don't watch out and I'll send that one to steal you away – that Sheikh Sín, the Thief of Thieves!'

Here, grey-haired but unquestionably scarred, was the notorious criminal himself – and was she out of her mind, were her ears playing tricks, or had he truly just announced that, given the stated circumstances, he himself was the only man for the job?

Struggling hard against the newborn goblins of nostalgia, Huma warned the fearsome volunteer that only a matter of extreme urgency and peril would have brought her unescorted into these ferocious streets.

'Because we can afford no last-minute backings-out,'

she continued, 'I am determined to tell you everything, keeping back no secrets whatsoever. If, after hearing me out, you are still prepared to proceed, then we shall do everything in our power to assist you, and to make you rich.'

The old thief shrugged, nodded, spat. Huma began her story.

Six days ago, everything in the household of her father, the wealthy moneylender Hashim, had been as it always was. At breakfast her mother had spooned khichri lovingly on to the moneylender's plate; the conversation had been filled with those expressions of courtesy and solicitude on which the family prided itself.

Hashim was fond of pointing out that while he was not a godly man he set great store by 'living honourably in the world'. In that spacious lakeside residence, all outsiders were greeted with the same formality and respect, even those unfortunates who came to negotiate for small fragments of Hashim's large fortune, and of whom he naturally asked an interest rate of over seventy per cent, partly, as he told his khichri-spooning wife, 'to teach these people the value of money; let them only learn that, and they will be cured of this fever of borrowing borrowing all the time – so you see that if my plans succeed, I shall put myself out of business!'

In their children, Atta and Huma, the moneylender and his wife had successfully sought to inculcate the virtues of thrift, plain dealing and a healthy independence of spirit. On this, too, Hashim was fond of congratulating himself.

Breakfast ended; the family members wished one another a fulfilling day. Within a few hours, however, the glassy contentment of that household, of that life of porcelain delicacy and alabaster sensibilities, was to be shattered beyond all hope of repair.

The moneylender summoned his personal shikara and was on the point of stepping into it when, attracted by a glint of silver, he noticed a small vial floating between the boat and his private quay. On an impulse, he scooped it out of the glutinous water.

It was a cylinder of tinted glass cased in exquisitely wrought silver, and Hashim saw within its walls a silver pendant bearing a single strand of human hair.

Closing his fist around this unique discovery, he muttered to the boatman that he'd changed his plans, and hurried to his sanctum, where, behind closed doors, he feasted his eyes on his find.

———

There can be no doubt that Hashim the moneylender knew from the first that he was in possession of the famous relic of the Prophet Muhammad, that revered hair whose theft from its shrine at Hazratbal mosque the previous morning had created an unprecedented hue and cry in the valley.

The thieves – no doubt alarmed by the pandemonium, by the procession through the streets of endless ululating crocodiles of lamentation, by the riots, the political ramifications and by the massive police search which was commanded and carried out by men whose entire careers now hung upon the finding of this lost hair – had evidently panicked and hurled the vial into the gelatine bosom of the lake.

Having found it by a stroke of great good fortune, Hashim's duty as a citizen was clear: the hair must be restored to its shrine, and the state to equanimity and peace.

But the moneylender had a different notion.

All around him in his study was the evidence of his collector's mania. There were enormous glass cases full of impaled butterflies from Gulmarg, three dozen scale models in various metals of the legendary cannon Zamzama, innumerable swords, a Naga spear, ninety-four terracotta camels of the sort sold on railway station platforms, many samovars, and a whole zoology of tiny sandalwood animals, which had originally been carved to serve as children's bathtime toys.

'And after all,' Hashim told himself, 'the Prophet would have disapproved mightily of this relic-worship. He abhorred the idea of being deified! So, by keeping this hair from its distracted devotees, I perform – do I not? – a finer service than I would by returning it! Naturally, I don't want it for its religious value . . . I'm a man of the world, of this world. I see it purely as a secular object of great rarity and blinding beauty. In short, it's the silver vial I desire, more than the hair.

'They say there are American millionaires who purchase stolen art masterpieces and hide them away – they would know how I feel. I must, must have it!'

Every collector must share his treasures with one other human being, and Hashim summoned – and told – his only son Atta, who was deeply perturbed but, having been sworn to secrecy, only spilled the beans when the troubles became too terrible to bear.

The youth excused himself and left his father alone in the crowded solitude of his collections. Hashim was sitting erect in a hard, straight-backed chair, gazing intently at the beautiful vial.

———

It was well known that the moneylender never ate lunch, so it was not until evening that a servant entered the sanctum to summon his master to the dining-table. He found Hashim as Atta had left him. The same, and not the same – for now the moneylender looked swollen, distended. His eyes bulged even more than they always had, they were red-rimmed, and his knuckles were white.

He seemed to be on the point of bursting! As though, under the influence of the misappropriated relic, he had filled up with some spectral fluid which might at any moment ooze uncontrollably from his every bodily opening.

He had to be helped to the table, and then the explosion did indeed take place.

Seemingly careless of the effect of his words on the carefully constructed and fragile constitution of the family's life, Hashim began to gush, to spume long streams of awful truths. In horrified silence, his children heard their father turn upon his wife, and reveal to her that for many years their marriage had been the worst of his afflictions. 'An end to politeness!' he thundered. 'An end to hypocrisy!'

Next, and in the same spirit, he revealed to his family the existence of a mistress; he informed them also of his

45

regular visits to paid women. He told his wife that, far from being the principal beneficiary of his will, she would receive no more than the eighth portion which was her due under Islamic law. Then he turned upon his children, screaming at Atta for his lack of academic ability – 'A dope! I have been cursed with a dope!' – and accusing his daughter of lasciviousness, because she went around the city barefaced, which was unseemly for any good Muslim girl to do. She should, he commanded, enter purdah forthwith.

Hashim left the table without having eaten and fell into the deep sleep of a man who has got many things off his chest, leaving his children stunned, in tears, and the dinner going cold on the sideboard under the gaze of an anticipatory bearer.

At five o'clock the next morning the moneylender forced his family to rise, wash and say their prayers. From then on, he began to pray five times daily for the first time in his life, and his wife and children were obliged to do likewise.

Before breakfast, Huma saw the servants, under her father's direction, constructing a great heap of books in the garden and setting fire to it. The only volume left untouched was the Qur'an, which Hashim wrapped in a silken cloth and placed on a table in the hall. He ordered each member of his family to read passages from this book for at least two hours per day. Visits to the cinema were forbidden. And if Atta invited male friends to the house, Huma was to retire to her room.

By now, the family had entered a state of shock and dismay; but there was worse to come.

That afternoon, a trembling debtor arrived at the house to confess his inability to pay the latest instalment of interest owed, and made the mistake of reminding Hashim, in somewhat blustering fashion, of the Qur'an's strictures against usury. The moneylender flew into a rage and attacked the fellow with one of his large collection of bullwhips.

By mischance, later the same day a second defaulter came to plead for time, and was seen fleeing Hashim's study with a great gash in his arm, because Huma's father had called him a thief of other men's money and had tried to cut off the wretch's right hand with one of the thirty-eight kukri knives hanging on the study walls.

These breaches of the family's unwritten laws of decorum alarmed Atta and Huma, and when, that evening, their mother attempted to calm Hashim down, he struck her on the face with an open hand. Atta leapt to his mother's defence and he, too, was sent flying.

'From now on,' Hashim bellowed, 'there's going to be some discipline around here!'

The moneylender's wife began a fit of hysterics which continued throughout that night and the following day, and which so provoked her husband that he threatened her with divorce, at which she fled to her room, locked the door and subsided into a raga of sniffling. Huma now lost her composure, challenged her father openly, and announced (with that same independence of spirit which he had encouraged in her) that she would wear no cloth over her face; apart from anything else, it was bad for the eyes.

On hearing this, her father disowned her on the spot and gave her one week in which to pack her bags and go.

By the fourth day, the fear in the air of the house had become so thick that it was difficult to walk around. Atta told his shock-numbed sister: 'We are descending to gutter-level – but I know what must be done.'

That afternoon, Hashim left home accompanied by two hired thugs to extract the unpaid dues from his two insolvent clients. Atta went immediately to his father's study. Being the son and heir, he possessed his own key to the moneylender's safe. This he now used, and removing the little vial from its hiding-place, he slipped it into his trouser pocket and re-locked the safe door.

Now he told Huma the secret of what his father had fished out of Lake Dal, and exclaimed: 'Maybe I'm crazy – maybe the awful things that are happening have made me cracked – but I am convinced there will be no peace in our house until this hair is out of it.'

His sister at once agreed that the hair must be returned, and Atta set off in a hired shikara to Hazrat-bal mosque. Only when the boat had delivered him into the throng of the distraught faithful which was swirling around the desecrated shrine did Atta discover that the relic was no longer in his pocket. There was only a hole, which his mother, usually so attentive to household matters, must have overlooked under the stress of recent events.

Atta's initial surge of chagrin was quickly replaced by a feeling of profound relief.

'Suppose', he imagined, 'that I had already announced to the mullahs that the hair was on my person! They would never have believed me now – and this mob would have lynched me! At any rate, it has gone, and that's a load off my mind.' Feeling more contented than he had for days, the young man returned home.

———

Here he found his sister bruised and weeping in the hall; upstairs, in her bedroom, his mother wailed like a brand-new widow. He begged Huma to tell him what had happened, and when she replied that their father, returning from his brutal business trip, had once again noticed a glint of silver between boat and quay, had once again scooped up the errant relic, and was consequently in a rage to end all rages, having beaten the truth out of her – then Atta buried his face in his hands and sobbed out his opinion, which was that the hair was persecuting them, and had come back to finish the job.

It was Huma's turn to think of a way out of their troubles.

While her arms turned black and blue and great stains spread across her forehead, she hugged her brother and whispered to him that she was determined to get rid of the hair *at all costs* – she repeated this last phrase several times.

'The hair', she then declared, 'was stolen from the mosque; so it can be stolen from this house. But it must be a genuine robbery, carried out by a bona-fide thief, not by one of us who are under the hair's thrall – by a thief so desperate that he fears neither capture nor curses.'

Unfortunately, she added, the theft would be ten times harder to pull off now that their father, knowing that there had already been one attempt on the relic, was certainly on his guard.

'Can you do it?'

Huma, in a room lit by candle and storm-lantern, ended her account with one further question: 'What assurances can you give that the job holds no terrors for you still?'

The criminal, spitting, stated that he was not in the habit of providing references, as a cook might, or a gardener, but he was not alarmed so easily, certainly not by any children's djinni of a curse. Huma had to be content with this boast, and proceeded to describe the details of the proposed burglary.

'Since my brother's failure to return the hair to the mosque, my father has taken to sleeping with his precious treasure under his pillow. However, he sleeps alone, and very energetically; only enter his room without waking him, and he will certainly have tossed and turned quite enough to make the theft a simple matter. When you have the vial, come to my room,' and here she handed Sheikh Sín a plan of her home, 'and I will hand over all the jewellery owned by my mother and myself. You will find . . . it is worth . . . that is, you will be able to get a fortune for it . . .'

It was evident that her self-control was weakening and that she was on the point of physical collapse.

'Tonight,' she burst out finally. 'You must come tonight!'

No sooner had she left the room than the old criminal's body was convulsed by a fit of coughing: he spat blood into an old vanaspati can. The great Sheikh, the 'Thief of Thieves', had become a sick man, and every day the time drew nearer when some young pretender to his power would stick a dagger in his stomach. A lifelong addiction to gambling had left him almost as poor as he had been when, decades ago, he had started out in this line of work as a mere pickpocket's apprentice; so in the extraordinary commission he had accepted from the moneylender's daughter he saw his opportunity of amassing enough wealth at a stroke to leave the valley for ever, and acquire the luxury of a respectable death which would leave his stomach intact.

As for the Prophet's hair, well, neither he nor his blind wife had ever had much to say for prophets – that was one thing they had in common with the moneylender's thunderstruck clan.

It would not do, however, to reveal the nature of this, his last crime, to his four sons. To his consternation, they had all grown up to be hopelessly devout men, who even spoke of making the pilgrimage to Mecca some day. 'Absurd!' their father would laugh at them. 'Just tell me how you will go?' For, with a parent's absolutist love, he had made sure they were all provided with a lifelong source of high income by crippling them at birth, so that, as they dragged themselves around the city, they earned excellent money in the begging business.

The children, then, could look after themselves.

He and his wife would be off soon with the jewel-boxes of the moneylender's women. It was a timely chance indeed that had brought the beautiful bruised girl into his corner of the town.

That night, the large house on the shore of the lake lay blindly waiting, with silence lapping at its walls. A burglar's night: clouds in the sky and mists on the winter water. Hashim the moneylender was asleep, the only member of his family to whom sleep had come that night. In another room, his son Atta lay deep in the coils of his coma with a blood-clot forming on his brain, watched over by a mother who had let down her long greying hair to show her grief, a mother who placed warm compresses on his head with gestures redolent of impotence. In a third bedroom Huma waited, fully dressed, amidst the jewel-heavy caskets of her desperation.

At last a bulbul sang softly from the garden below her window and, creeping downstairs, she opened a door to the bird, on whose face there was a scar in the shape of the Nastaliq letter *sín*.

Noiselessly, the bird flew up the stairs behind her. At the head of the staircase they parted, moving in opposite directions along the corridor of their conspiracy without a glance at one another.

Entering the moneylender's room with professional ease, the burglar, Sín, discovered that Huma's predictions had been wholly accurate. Hashim lay sprawled diagonally across his bed, the pillow untenanted by his head, the prize easily accessible. Step by padded step, Sín moved towards the goal.

It was at this point that, in the bedroom next door, young Atta sat bolt upright in his bed, giving his mother a great fright, and without any warning – prompted by goodness knows what pressure of the blood-clot upon his brain – began screaming at the top of his voice:

'*Thief! Thief! Thief!*'

———

It seems probable that his poor mind had been dwelling, in these last moments, upon his own father; but it is impossible to be certain, because having uttered these three emphatic words the young man fell back upon his pillow and died.

At once his mother set up a screeching and a wailing and a keening and a howling so earsplittingly intense that they completed the work which Atta's cry had begun – that is, her laments penetrated the walls of her husband's bedroom and brought Hashim wide awake.

Sheikh Sín was just deciding whether to dive beneath the bed or brain the moneylender good and proper when Hashim grabbed the tiger-striped swordstick which always stood propped up in a corner beside his bed, and rushed from the room without so much as noticing the burglar who stood on the opposite side of the bed in the darkness. Sín stooped quickly and removed the vial containing the Prophet's hair from its hiding-place.

Meanwhile Hashim had erupted into the corridor, having unsheathed the sword inside his cane. In his right hand he held the weapon and was waving it about dementedly. His left hand was shaking the stick. A shadow came rushing towards him through the midnight darkness of the passageway and, in his somnolent anger, the moneylender thrust his sword fatally through its heart. Turning up the light, he found that he had murdered his daughter, and under the dire influence of this accident he was so overwhelmed by remorse that he turned the sword upon himself, fell upon it and so extinguished his life. His wife, the sole surviving member of the family, was driven mad by the general carnage and had to be committed to an asylum for the insane by her brother, the city's Deputy Commissioner of Police.

Sheikh Sín had quickly understood that the plan had gone awry.

Abandoning the dream of the jewel-boxes when he was but a few yards from its fulfilment, he climbed out of Hashim's window and made his escape during the appalling events described above. Reaching home before dawn, he woke his wife and confessed his failure. It would be necessary, he whispered, for him to vanish for a while. Her blind eyes never opened until he had gone.

The noise in the Hashim household had roused their servants and even managed to awaken the night-watchman, who had been fast asleep as usual on his charpoy by the street-gate. They alerted the police, and the Deputy Commissioner himself was informed. When he heard of Huma's death, the mournful officer opened and read the sealed letter which his niece had given him, and instantly led a large detachment of armed men into the light-repellent gullies of the most wretched and disreputable part of the city.

The tongue of a malicious cat-burglar named Huma's fellow-conspirator; the finger of an ambitious bank-robber pointed at the house in which he lay concealed; and although Sín managed to crawl through a hatch in the attic and attempt a roof-top escape, a bullet from the Deputy Commissioner's own rifle penetrated his stomach and brought him crashing messily to the ground at the feet of Huma's enraged uncle.

From the dead thief's pocket rolled a vial of tinted glass, cased in filigree silver.

The recovery of the Prophet's hair was announced at once on All-India Radio. One month later, the valley's holiest men assembled at the Hazratbal mosque and formally authenticated the relic. It sits to this day in a closely guarded vault by the shores of the loveliest of lakes in the heart of the valley which was once closer than any other place on earth to Paradise.

———

But before our story can properly be concluded, it is necessary to record that when the four sons of the dead Sheikh awoke on the morning of his death, having unwittingly spent a few minutes under the same roof as the famous hair, they found that a miracle had occurred, that they were all sound of limb and strong of wind, as whole as they might have been if their father had not thought to smash their legs in the first hours of their lives. They were, all four of them, very properly furious, because the miracle had reduced their earning powers by 75 per cent, at the most conservative estimate; so they were ruined men.

Only the Sheikh's widow had some reason for feeling grateful, because although her husband was dead she had regained her sight, so that it was possible for her to spend her last days gazing once more upon the beauties of the valley of Kashmir.

WEST

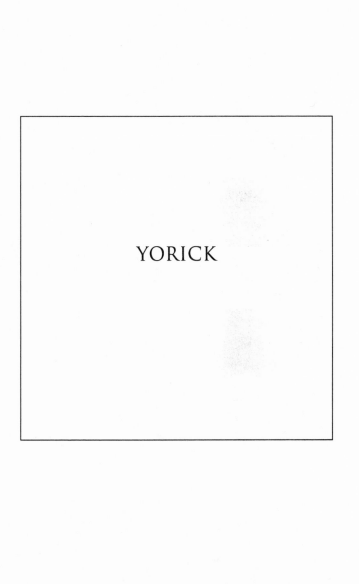

YORICK

Thank the heavens! – or the diligence of ancient-time papersmiths – for the existence upon our earth of the material known as *strong vellum*; which, like the earth upon which I have supposed it to exist (although in point of fact its contacts with *terra firma* are most rare, its natural habitations being shelves, wooden or not wooden, some dusty, others maintained in excellent order; or letter-boxes, desk drawers, old trunks, the most secret pockets of courting lovers, shops, files, attics, cellars, museums, deed-boxes, safes, lawyers' offices, doctors' walls, your favourite great-aunt's sea-side home, theatrical property departments, fairy tales, summit conferences, tourist traps), . . . like the earth, I say again in case you have forgot my purpose, this noble stuff endures – if not for ever, then at least till men consciously destroy it, whether by crumpling or shredding, through the use of kitchen scissors or strong teeth, by actions incendiary or lavatorial, – for it's a true fact that men take an equal pleasure in annihilating both the ground upon which they stand while they live and the substance (I mean paper) upon which they may remain, immortalised, once this same ground is over their heads instead of under their feet; and that the complete inventory of such strategies of destruction would over-fill more pages than my ration, . . . so then to the devil with that list and on with my story; which, as I had begun to say, is itself the tale of a piece of vellum, – both the tale of the vellum itself and the tale inscribed thereupon.

Yorick's saga, of course; that same ancient account which fell, near enough two hundred and thirty-five years ago, into the hands of a certain – no, a most uncertain – *Tristram*, who (although Yseult-less) was neither triste nor ram, the frothiest, most heady Shandy of a fellow; and which has now come into my possession by processes too arcane to detain the eager reader. Truly, a velluminous history! – which it's my present intent not merely to abbreviate, but, in addition, to explicate, annotate, hyphenate, palatinate & permanganate – for it's a narrative that richly rewards the scholar who is competent to apply such sensitive technologies. Here, dusty-faced and inky-fingered, lurk beautiful young wives, old fools, cuckoldry, jealousy, murder, juice of cursed hebona, executions, skulls; as well as a full exposition of why, in the *Hamlet* of William Shakespeare, the morbid prince seems unaware of his own father's real name.

Very well then: –

It appears that in the latter part of the reign of the illustrious King *Horwendillus* of Denmark, his chief jester, one Master YORICK, took to wife a toothsome goldhair waif, by name 'Ophelia'; and thereafter began all the trouble . . . What's this? Interruptions already? Did I not tell you, have I not just this moment set down, that the bardic Hamlet, that's to say Amlethus of the Danes, is quite mistaken in believing the Ghost's name to be Hamlet too? – An error not only unusual but unfilial, not only unfilial but downright *unsaxogrammatical*, one may say, for it is contradicted by no less an authority than Saxo-Grammaticus's *History of the Danes*! – But were you to be silent and hear me out you'd learn it was no mistake whatsoever, but rather the cryptic key by which our tale's true meaning may most swiftly be unlocked.

I repeat: –

Horwendillus. Horwendillus Rex . . . – Still more questions? – Sir, of course the jester had a wife; she may not feature in the great man's play, but you'll concede that a woman's a necessary apparatus if a man would make a dynasty, and how else? – answer me that? – could the antique Fool have produced that Line, that veritable Monologue of Yoricks of whom the ill-named Tristram person's *parson* was but one single syllable? Well! You don't need ancient vellum to see the truth of THAT, I think. – Good Lord; her *name*? Sir, you must take it upon my word. But where's the puzzle? Do you imagine that this 'Ophelia' was so blasted uncommon a name in a land where men were called such things as Amlethus, Horwend&c., yes, and Yorick, too? So, so. Let's get on.

Yorick espoused Ophelia. There was a child. Let's have no more disputes.

In the matter of this Ophelia: she'd less than half his years and more than twice his looks, so it will instantly be perceived that what follows may be ascribed to divisions and multiplications. An arithmetical tragedy, in sum. A grave tale, fit for gravesides.

How did it come about that this old wintry fool got himself such a springtime of a bride? – A noisome gale blows across the ancient vellum hereabouts. It is Ophelia's breath. The rottenest-smelling exhalation in the State of Denmark; a tepid stench of rats' livers, toads' piss, high game-birds, rotting teeth, gangrene, skewered corpses, burning witchflesh, sewers, politicians' consciences, skunk-holes, sepulchres, and all the Beelzebubbling pickle-vats of Hell! Thus every time this youthful beauty, the frail perfection of whose features brought moisture to men's eyes, made so bold as to open her mouth, – why, then there was cleared all around her an open ground some fifty feet in radius at

the least. So Yorick's path to wedlock was unob-
structed, and a poor Fool must get what wife he can.

He courted her with a wooden peg on his nose. On
their wedding day the king, who loved Yorick, gave the
jester a thoughtful gift: a pair of silver nose-plugs.
That's how it happened; first pegged, then plugged, our
Fool in love assuredly looked his part.

So that's made clear.

[*Enter young Prince Amlethus, bearing a riding
whip.*]

The scene's a poor bedchamber at Elsinore. Yorick and
his lady lie fast asleep in their cot. In disarray upon a
nearby chair: a cap, bells, motley, &c. Somewhere,
a sleeping infant. Picture the boy Hamlet now, tip-
toeing to the bedside; where he tenses, crouched; until
at last he leaps! And now,

Yor. (awakes) O, a! What whoreson Pelion's this,
that, tumbling down from Ossa, so interrupts my spine?

. . . I interrupt myself, for there occurs to me a discor-
dant Note: would any man, awakened from deepest
slumber by the arrival on his back of a seven-year-old
princeling, truly retain such a command of metaphor
and classical allusion as is indicated by the text? It may
be that the vellum is not wholly to be relied upon in this
regard; or it may be that Denmark's fools were most

uncommon learned. Some things may never be known . . .

(Back now to our Muttons.)

Ham. Yorick, the day's awake! Let's raise a chorus to the dawn.

Oph. (aside) My husband never loved this prince; a spoiled short brat, and cursed with sleeplessness, which plague he passes on to us. Here's how we wake each morning, with royal fists a-tearing at our hair, or heir-apparent buttocks jig-jogging on our necks. Were he my child . . . good morrow, sweet my prince!

Ham. Ophelia, it is. A dawn chorus, Yorick, come!

Yor. That's for the birds. I'm of too venerable feather, that's the truth. My years long since encrowed me, or made of me an owl. I sing no more, but only caw or hoot in most unseemly form.

Ham. Soft! None of this. Your prince would have a song.

Yor. Still hear me out. Age, Hamlet, is a setting sun, and in my occidental years it is not right I hymn the orient day.

Ham. No more. Up, sing. I'll ride upon your back and hear you croon.

Oph. (aside) At seven he's the Old Man of the Sea; who knows, at twenty-seven, what he'll be?

Yor. (sings) *In youth when I did love, did love,*

Methought it was very sweet, To contract, O! the time, for-a my behove, O! methought there was nothing meet. But age, with his stealing steps, Hath claw'd me in his clutch . . .

Ham. Cease, Yorick, this foul caterwaul; instanter, hold your peace.

Yor. Did I not tell you true?

Ham. Enough. Give me some jest. Yes, make it about a cat, just such a wauly mog as you just now surpassed.

Yor. (aside) Now must I do this penance for doing what he willed. (Aloud) There's life yet in this old dog you ride; so tell me, Hamlet, why cats have nine lives?

Ham. I know it not, but why they have nine tails, that I know well, and you shall find it out quick if the riddle be slow.

Oph. (aside) This prince is as sharp as his tongue; and poor Yorick blunter by the day.

Yor. Then hear the answer. All cats will look at kings; but to gaze upon a monarch is to place one's life in their hands; and lives held in such hands do often slip through fingers and are spilled. Now, Hamlet, count the spaces on your hands, I mean 'twixt finger and finger, and finger and finger, and finger and finger, and finger and thumb. On two hands, count eight chasms through which a life may fall. Only nine lives will ensure that one at least remain; and so our cat, king-watching, must have nine.

Oph. Husband, a fine conceit.

Ham. So now a dance! Discharge your jester's office and let's have a merry jig.

Yor. You'll hang upon my back the while?

Ham. I will; there to ponder what I want.

Yor. (aside, and dancing) Hamlet, you want for nothing: yet Yorick finds you wanting.

And all this spoken with filigree'd plugs up the nose, up princely nostrils as well as Foolish ones! – The child, crying in his cradle, complains as much of his bunged proboscis as of the noise of Hamlet's whip, whishing and whooshing through the air to encourage his dancing biped steed. – What are we to think of so enraged a prince? It's sure he hated Ophelia; but for what? Her pestilential gusts? Her sovereignty over the Fool, who doted upon her very eyelashes? Or could it have been the swelling buds beneath her shift, her body that was not his to command? At seven, Prince Amlethus is disturbed by something in this girl, but cannot give it name. – So childish ardour turns to hate.

Perhaps all three: her stink; her theft of Yorick's heart, for as any fool knows the heart of a Fool is his prince's possession, for who but a Fool would surrender his heart to a prince?; and, yes, her beauty, too. There's no need to choose. Let's be gluttonous in our understanding and swallow this trinity whole.

We shall spare Hamlet too harsh a judgment. He was a lonely child, who saw in Yorick a father as well as a servant, viz. the best, the perfect father, for every son would make his father a slave. In Yorick, singing, jesting, dancing, the pallid prince sees Horwendillus tamed. He was a mother's boy.

The vellum hereabouts, – I should say the ink upon it – or, more precisely still, the fist that held the pen – but the fist's long dead, and it won't do to speak ill of the departed – O, **********!, let me say *the text* begins to ramble, listing in gruesome detail all the crimes committed by the prince against the jester's person: each imprint of royal boot upon his buttocks, complete with itemisations of cause, effect, location, costume, contingent circumstances (rain, sun, thundery conditions, hail, and other functions of nature; or the absence of Hamlet's mother owing to the tyranny, even over queens, of natural functions), descriptions of the jester's pratfalls, of the clump of turf with which his nose collided, of subsequent searches for dislodged noseplugs; in brief, a most lamentable lack of brevity, which we shall rectify here without delay. The point's well made, I think. To labour it further would be to emulate the prince, who belaboured Yorick with sticks and whips and the Lord knows what – and we would be rash to treat our Reader (being ourselves no Prince) as if he were a Fool. (And being no Prince, what business have I with this newly infiltrative 'we', this purple plural my sentences have presumed to put on? Off with it! Back to the common – the *uncommon*, because *Cyclopean* – singular I.)

One story will suffice:-

While riding Yorick, Hamlet with his whip parted the fool's cheek's fleshy curtains, to reveal the bony stage behind. It seems he was a feeling prince: enshouldered as he was, his gorge rose at the bloody sight. – Reader, the Prince of Denmark, on catching his first glimpse of a skull, puked generously on Yorick's dingling cap.

I have till now endeavoured to tell a delicate tale of private character, with many fine touches of psychology and much material detail; still I can no longer keep the great World from my pages, for what ended in Tragedy began in Politics. (Which will be small surprise.)

Picture a banquet at fabulous Elsinore: boar's heads, sheep's eyes, parson's noses, goose-breasts, calves' livers, tripes, fish-roes, venison haunches, pig's trotters

(here's the anatomy of the table; were its several dishes assembled into a single edible beast, a stranger monster would lie here than any hippogriff or ichthyocentaur!).
– Tonight Horwendillus and his *Gertrude* are feasting FORTINBRAS, hoping to stay his territorial greed by satisfying his belly's equal liking for expansion, the latter requiring no more than the murder of the above mythical monster, a happier & certainly a tastier Strategy than **WAR**.

And is it not conceivable that *F.*, seeing upon the laden board the dismembered limbs of this fearsomely diverse and most occult of creatures, and constructing in his mind's eye the whole composite Beast, with antlers on its giant turkey's head, and hooves set weirdly down beneath its scaly belly and its hairy shanks, might lose all appetite for the fray – fearing to confront on Danish battlefields the mighty race of hunters who could slay so wild a Thing – and might therefore cease to hunger for Denmark herself?

It does not matter. I've lingered at the banquet only to explain why this Queen Gertrude, over-occupied by diplomacy, beset by several types of meat, was unable to go upstairs and wish her son goodnight.

I must show you Hamlet sleepless in his bed, – but where's the fellow who can portray an absence? – of

sleep, I mean, and of a mother's kiss upon his cheek, –
for a cheek unkissed resembles in all particulars a
cheek for which no osculation had been hoped, and
a boy shewn horizontal in his cot, and subject to the
tergiversations & other Frenzies characteristic of
insomnia, may nevertheless be taken for a child plagued
by a flea; or fevered; or surly, at being forbidden the
grown-ups' table; or practising his swimming in this
textile sea; or G— knows what, for I don't. But absence,
as is well known, makes hearts grow fonder; so up
Amlethus gets, and tip-toes down corridors thus (if
each dot represent the conjunction of one toe-tip with
the floor):

. . . . ./ . . . . ./ . . . . ./ . . . . ./ . . . . ./, &c. &c.

– until (to be as brisk as he) he reaches Gertrude's
chamber, rushes in, and resolves to await her there, so
that what's missing from his cheek may be presented; a
Lethe-kiss from Mother, and then he'll sleep.

(As it turned out, this proved a lethal scheme.)

And now, in pantomime, let me display what followed
(for I'm afraid my pages' mean allotment may expire
before my tale, and so in compensation for my earlier
garrulity these my characters may be obliged to rush
through Dumb-Shows, *tableaux*, and other acceleratory
devices quite unsuited to the story's tragic content. But

there is nothing for it; my present long-winded Folly must make these ancients Fools. Thus haste, enforced by our inevitable end, makes **Yoricks** of us all):–

Hamlet Aghast: There are voices at the door! Not only his mother's, but some fierce drunken sot's! – Quick, hide! – But where? – The arras, not a moment to be lost! – He hides. (And so it may be said of him that in later life he slew himself, his child-self's memory lurking in this place, grown hoary and Polonial in form.)

O, what he hears! The grunting, roaring man! His mother's squeals and shrieks – ah, frail maternal cries! – Who threatens the Queen? – Bravely, the prince peers round the arras' edge, and sees . . .

. . . *HIS FATHER* falling wild upon the lady. It is a porky-snuffling Horwendillo beneath whom Queen Gertrude sobs and flails, – and then falls quiet, while her breath sounds harsh in Hamlet's ears, as if her throat were stopped.

The prince hears Death upon her voice, and understands, with a seven-year-old's acuteness, that his father's bent on murder.

Now out he leaps!

'Stop! Stop, I say!'

His father's springing back! His mother's hand flies to her throat, confirming Hamlet's fears of throttling!

The scene is plain enough. 'I saved her life,' Amlethus proudly thinks. – But drunken Horwendillus takes his son, & thrashes him, & lashes, & then thrashes once again. – A curious sort of thrashing, for it beats something into the prince's hide, – whereas the nature of most punishment is to beat an evil out.

What's beaten in? Why, hatred; and dark dreams of revenge.

Hamlet Alone: But I'll leave soliloquies to richer pens. My vellum's silent on what Hamlet felt while locked & wealy in his room. You must infer his thoughts from what he did.

If you desire, you may see him haunted. A Horwendillian phantom shimmers before his eyes and seems to squeeze the life-breath from the Queen. Amlethus's eyes, made visionary by fear, observe the dreadful Spectre as it assassinates Queen Gertrude a thousand times and more, now falling upon her to choke her in the bath (soap-bubbles die upon her lip), now strangling her at her mirror, so forcing her to watch her own Demise.

Reader, see Hamlet's dreams: look through his eyes at Horwendillus's chimaera, its fingers at his mother's throat, in gardens, kitchens, ballrooms and potting-sheds; on chairs, beds, tables & floors; in public and in private, by day and by night, before and after luncheon, while she sings and when she is silent, clothed and nude, in boats and on horseback, enthroned or upon her piss-pot . . . and you may understand why he, the prince, now sees his recent 'rescue' as no End, but only a Beginning, to his loving anguish; why he racks his brains to find some permanent conclusion to his fear. – And so a *Plot* is born, conceived by Urgency out of Hate, its generative organ the royal whip that stung his royal buttocks, delivering upon those nether cheeks just such a yoricking as he'd often given the Fool.

And the plot begins to converge on Yorick; bitter Hamlet will use the jester as his revenge's tool.

Now you may see two hatreds coalesce: in Hamlet's angry brain his fury merges (one might as well say *marries*) Ophelia and the King. He sees how his hard wrath can stone down both these birds (for it is a Medusan wrath, that can turn yoric flesh to deadly granite).

And, at last, you hear the child-prince in his room, walking round & round about, a sullen riddle dripping from his lips: –

'Nor *liquid, nor solid, nor gassy air,*
Nor taste, nor smell, nor substance there.
It may be turned to good or ill.
Pour it in an ear, and it may kill.'

– So, Reader, my congratulations. Your fancy, from which all these dark suppositions have issued (for I began this passage by swearing myself to silence), is proved by them more fertile & convincing than my own.

So well, so accurately have you supposed that my task's made very brief. It remains only to bring Hamlet and Yorick, the one upon the other's back as is their custom, to a Platform below the Castle at Elsinore; – where the young prince pours such a magical poison into Yorick's ear that the Fool falls into foolish Delusions.

You have understood it all. – The ghost of Hamlet's living father appears, to haunt poor Yorick; and the venom conjures up a second undead phantasm – it is Ophelia, Yorick's wife, her clothes in disarray, her body twined in translucent, ectoplasmic splendour round the King's!

– *What was the princely poison?* –

Only solve your own riddle, Reader, and you'll know . . . there, never mind, I'll solve it for you. It was SPEECH.

O deadliest venene! Being insubstantial, though very serpentine, it knows no antidote. – To be plain, Hamlet persuades his father's Fool that Horwendillus and Ophelia, that Dame Yorick and the King . . . no, I cannot say that terrible word of doing, when in truth was nothing done! – And possibly (the vellum is smudged, at this point, by ancient tears or other salty fluid) the cruel boy brought 'proofs': – a pair of golden nose-plugs, wrapped in a forged billet-doux? Or was it a handkerchief? No matter. The damage is done, and Yorick is multiply a fool: always a Fool by trade, he has become a doubled Dolt for being the Prince's *gull*, and (in his own eyes, for, as he sees it, seeming a Fool in the lovers' eyes) an Ass as well, an Ass most Foolish in appearance, because of the cuckold's horns between his ears.

Strangest of all – and here's the dark heart of the matter – by becoming a Fool-Actual, he sacrifices the privileges of the Fool-Professional. A jester was a curious brand of Fool, permitted by his motley to speak wisdom and have men laugh at it; to tell the truth, yet keep his head, jingling as it was with silly bells. – Yes, Fools were wise, as wise as clocks, for they knew their time for what it was. – But now this clock-wise Yorick changes round; fooled by the prince, he starts to play the Fool – to play it truly, that's to say to rant, to roar, to act the jealous spouse in deadly seriousness.

Which was Hamlet's intention: to force the Fool into a fatal folly. I've said he saw the jester as a second, clownish father: this surrogate parent is now by poisoned words unleashed against the royal sire.

For the rest: –

Horwendillus sleeps alone in his Gethsemane. Enter Yorick, with juices of cursed hebona in a phial. – The poison Hamlet poured into his ear has precipitated, or so it fancifully seems, into this bottle; – and from the bottle into the king's ear it goes. – And that's Horwendillus dead; while Ophelia, accused and spurned by Yorick, loses her senses and wanders round the palace in a flowery madness until she dies of grief; – which madness gives the clue to Claudius, who then uncovers the crime, and it's to the block with Yorick, and that's that.

– But here's a mystery, an unknown hand at work! For *someone*, whom I cannot name, retrieves the Sever'd Head; and with all necessary bribes and whispers secretly contrives to have it buried there, where after many years the prince will be confronted by his grinning bony guilt. – So a faceless joker, some lover of the jester's heady wit, makes of his discarded noodle a most 'capital' (if unforeseen) amusement.

Tumpty tum, tumpty tum, and a tumpty tumpty tum ... Reader, time's passing, and each of us passes the time in his own sweet way, whether by drumming

of fingers, or in sleep, or courtship, or the consumption of strings of sausages, or however we please; my
own habit is to hum, and so tum tum tumpty tum. (If
the tune distress you, be off and pass the time in some
other place; freedom's a spaniel that grows weak and
flabby if it be not exercised, so exercise your dog, Sir,
that's the trick.)

– But, returning after many years to our Scene, what
is this we see? Not Yorick; he's dead. Then, *YORICK'S
GHOST*. For he seems to haunt the living, so that we
may call him Will-o'-the-Wits . . . Reader, how much
has gone wrong at Elsinore!

Gertrude, murderously 'rescued' by her son from
her first, un-murderous spouse, remained in mourning
many years, while Claudius ruled. (In this it's true my
history differs from Master CHACKPAW's, and ruins
at least one great soliloquy. I offer no defence, but this:
that these matters are shrouded in antiquity, and there's
no certainty in them; so let the versions of the story co-
exist, for there's no need to choose. – Or this: that
when Queen Gertrude at last did marry Claudius, the
intervening years were, in Hamlet's troubled mind, by
this action concertina'ed, blurred together, compressed;
so that to him the passage of his childhood, adolescence
and young manhood appeared no longer than two
months [nay, not so much, not two] . . . and this is

wholly comprehensible, for have they not flown by in the brief space of time it took to sing my tumpty tum? Have they not passed in the few moments it took to walk *Freedom*, your spaniel bitch? – Well, then, you have two unanswerable cases instead of one; and that's enough, I hope.)

As I was saying: Gertrude marries! And now dead Yorick's jealousy, unhoused from the jester's corpse and seeking a new home, finds one in Hamlet. 'Tis clear – so Hamlet plots – that King Claudius must be accused of his brother's murder, and Yorick's execution must be shown to be the camouflage, the *arras* behind which the Truth was hid. – So Murder's spectre is invoked a second time, and Hamlet, in his mother-loving passion, sees it walk the battlements of Elsinore.

But this Ghost bears his own name: by which the prince, the accuser, is accused. Haunted by the Phantom of his crime, he starts to lose his reason. His own *Ophelia* he treats badly, as you know; his cracking brain confuses her with the unbearable memory of the Fool's falsely maligned and foully odorous wife; until at last the prince, who once turned Speech to Poison, drinks from a poisoned cup . . . and then dead marches, and also marches of the living:– old Fortinbras, too long uninvited to a meal, gobbles Denmark up instead.

———

Yorick's child survives, and leaves the scene of his family's tragedy; wanders the world, sowing his seed in far-off lands, from west to east and back again; and multicoloured generations follow, ending (I'll now reveal) in this present, humble *AUTHOR*; whose ancestry may be proved by this, which he holds in common with the whole sorry line of the family, that his chief weakness is for the telling of a particular species of Tale, which learned men have termed *chanticleric*, and also *taurean*.

– And just such a COCK-AND-BULL story is by this last confession brought quite to its conclusion.

AT THE AUCTION OF
THE RUBY SLIPPERS

The bidders who have assembled for the auction of the magic slippers bear little resemblance to your usual saleroom crowd. The Auctioneers have publicised the event widely and are prepared for all comers. People venture out but rarely nowadays; nevertheless, and rightly, the Auctioneers believed this prize would tempt us from our bunkers. High feelings are anticipated. Accordingly, in addition to the standard facilities provided for the comfort and security of the more notable personages, extra-large bronze cuspidors have been placed in the vestibules and toilets, for the use of the physically sick; teams of psychiatrists of varying disciplines have been installed in strategically located neo-Gothic confessional booths, to counsel the sick at heart.

Most of us nowadays are sick.

There are no priests. The Auctioneers have drawn a line. The priests remain in other, nearby buildings, buildings with which they are familiar, hoping to deal with any psychic fall-out, any insanity overspill.

Units of obstetricians and helmeted police SWAT teams wait out of sight in side alleys in case the excitement leads to unexpected births or deaths. Lists of next of kin have been drawn up and their contact numbers recorded. A supply of strait-jackets has been laid in.

See: behind bullet-proof glass, the ruby slippers sparkle. We do not know the limits of their powers. We suspect that these limits may not exist.

Movie stars are here, among the bidders, bringing their glossy, spangled auras to the saleroom. Movie-star auras, developed in collaboration with masters of Applied Psychics, are platinum, golden, silver, bronze. Certain genre actors specialising in villainous rôles are surrounded by auras of evil – livid green, mustard yellow, inky red. When one of us collides with a star's priceless (and fragile) aura, he or she is instantly knocked to the floor by a security team and hustled out to the waiting paddy-wagons. Such incidents slightly reduce the crush in the Grand Saleroom.

The memorabilia junkies are out in predictable force, and now with a ducking movement of the head one of them applies her desperate lips to the slippers' transparent cage, setting off the state-of-the-art defence system whose programmers have neglected to teach it about the relative harmlessness of such a gesture of adoration. The system pumps a hundred thousand volts of electricity into the collagen-implanted lips of the glass-kisser, terminating her interest in the proceedings.

It is an unpleasantly whiffy moment, but it fails to deter a second *aficionado* from the same suicidal act of devotion. When we learn that this moron was the lover of the first fatality, we rather wonder at the mysteries of love, whilst reaching once again for our perfumed handkerchiefs.

The cult of the ruby slippers is at its height. A fancy dress party is in full swing. Wizards, Lions, Scarecrows are in plentiful supply. They jostle crossly for position, stamping on one another's feet. There is a scarcity of Tin Men on account of the particular discomfort of the costume. Witches bide their time on the *balcons* and *galeries* of the Grand Saleroom, living gargoyles with, in many cases, high credit ratings. One corner is occupied entirely by Totos, several of whom are copulating enthusiastically, obliging a rubber-gloved janitor to separate them so as to avoid giving public offence. He does this with great delicacy and taste.

We, the public, are easily, lethally offended. We have come to think of taking offence as a fundamental right. We value very little more highly than our rage, which gives us, in our opinion, the moral high ground. From this high ground we can shoot down at our enemies and inflict heavy fatalities. We take pride in our short fuses. Our anger elevates, transcends.

Around the – let us say – shrine of the ruby-sequinned slippers, pools of saliva have been forming. There are those of us who lack restraint, who drool. The jump-suited Latino janitor moves amongst us, a pail in one hand and a squeegee mop in the other. We admire and are grateful for his talent for self-effacement. He removes our mouth waters from the floor without causing any loss of face on our part.

Opportunities for encountering the truly miraculous are limited in our Nietzschean, relativistic universe. Behaviourist philosophers and quantum scientists crowd around the magic shoes. They make indecipherable notes.

Exiles, displaced persons of all sorts, even homeless tramps have turned up for a glimpse of the impossible. They have emerged from their subterranean hollows and braved the bazookas, the Uzi-armed gangs high on crack or smack or ice, the smugglers, the emptiers of houses. The tramps wear stenchy jute ponchos and hawk noisily into the giant potted yuccas. They grab fistfuls of canapés from trays borne upon the superb palms of A-list caterers. Sushi is eaten by them with impressive quantities of *wasabi* sauce, to whose inflammatory powers the hoboes' innards seem impervious. SWAT teams are summoned and after a brief battle involving the use of rubber bullets and sedative darts the tramps are removed, clubbed into unconsciousness and driven away. They will be deposited some distance beyond the city limits, out there in that smoking no-man's-land surrounded by giant advertising hoardings into which we venture no more. Wild dogs will gather around them, eager for luncheon. These are uncompromising times.

Political refugees are at the auction: conspirators, deposed monarchs, defeated factions, poets, bandit chieftains. Such figures no longer wear the black berets, the pebble-lensed spectacles and enveloping greatcoats of yesteryear, but strike resplendent attitudes in boxy silken jackets and high-waisted Japanese couture pantaloons. The women sport toreador jackets bearing sequinned representations of great works of art. One beauty parades *Guernica* on her back, while several others wear glittering scenes from the *Disasters of War* sequence by Francisco Goya.

Incandescent as they are in their suits of lights, the

female political refugees fail to eclipse the ruby slippers, and huddle with their male comrades in small hissing bunches, periodically hurling imprecations, ink-pellets, spitballs and paper darts across the salon at rival clusters of *émigrés*. The guards at the exits crack their bullwhips idly and the politicals control themselves.

We revere the ruby slippers because we believe they can make us invulnerable to witches (and there are so many sorcerers pursuing us nowadays); because of their powers of reverse metamorphosis, their affirmation of a lost state of normalcy in which we have almost ceased to believe and to which the slippers promise us we can return; and because they shine like the footwear of the gods.

Disapproving critiques of the fetishising of the slippers are offered by religious fundamentalists, who have been allowed to gain entry by virtue of the extreme liberalism of some of the Auctioneers, who argue that a civilised saleroom must be a broad church, open, tolerant. The fundamentalists have openly stated that they are interested in buying the magic footwear only in order to burn it, and this is not, in the view of the liberal Auctioneers, a reprehensible programme. What price tolerance if the intolerant are not tolerated also?

'Money insists on democracy,' the liberal Auctioneers insist. 'Anyone's cash is as good as anyone else's.' The fundamentalists fulminate from soap-boxes constructed of special, sanctified wood. They are ignored, but some senior figures present speak ominously of the thin end of the wedge.

Orphans arrive, hoping that the ruby slippers might transport them back through time as well as space (for, as our equations prove, all space machines are time machines as well): they hope to be reunited with their deceased parents by the famous shoes.

Men and women of dubious character are present – untouchables, outcasts. The security forces deal brusquely with many of these.

'Home' has become such a scattered, damaged, various concept in our present travails. There is so much to yearn for. There are so few rainbows any more. How hard can we expect even a pair of magic shoes to work? They promised to take us *home*, but are metaphors of homeliness comprehensible to them, are abstractions permissible? Are they literalists, or will they permit us to redefine the blessed word?

Are we asking, hoping for, too much?

As our numberless needs emerge from their redoubts

and press in upon the electrified glass, will the shoes, like the Grimms' ancient flatfish, lose patience with our ever-growing demands and return us to the hovels of our discontents?

The presence of imaginary beings in the Saleroom may be the last straw. Children from nineteenth-century Australian paintings are here, whining from their ornate, gilded frames about being lost in the immensity of the Outback. In blue smocks and ankle socks they gaze into rain forests and red deserts, and tremble.

A literary character, condemned to an eternity of reading the works of Dickens to an armed madman in a jungle, has sent in a written bid.

On a television monitor, I notice the frail figure of an alien creature with an illuminated fingertip.

This permeation of the real world by the fictional is a symptom of the moral decay of our post-millennial culture. Heroes step down off cinema screens and marry members of the audience. Will there be no end to it? Should there be more rigorous controls? Is the State employing insufficient violence? We debate such questions often. There can be little doubt that a large majority of us opposes the free, unrestricted migration of imaginary beings into an already damaged reality, whose resources diminish by the day. After all, few of us would choose to travel in the opposite direction (though there are persuasive reports of an increase in such migrations latterly).

I shelve such disputes for the moment. The Auction is about to begin.

It is necessary that I speak about my cousin Gale, and her habit of moaning loudly while making love. Let me be frank: my cousin Gale was and is the love of my life, and even now that we have parted I am easily aroused by the mere memory of her erotic noisiness. I hasten to add that except for this volubility there was nothing abnormal about our love-making, nothing, if I may put it thus, *fictional*. Yet it satisfied me deeply, deeply, especially when she chose to cry out at the moment of penetration: 'Home, boy! Home, baby, yes – you've come home!'

One day, sad to relate, I came home to find her in the arms of a hairy escapee from a caveman movie. I moved out the same day, weeping my way down the street with my portrait of Gale in the guise of a tornado cradled in my arms and my collection of old Pat Boone 78 r.p.m. records in a rucksack on my back.

This happened many years ago.

For a time after Gale dumped me I was bitter and would reveal to our social circle that she had lost her virginity at the age of fourteen in an accident involving a defective shooting-stick; but vindictiveness did not satisfy me for long.

Since those days I have dedicated myself to her memory. I have made of myself a candle at her temple.

I am aware that, after all these years of separation and non-communication, the Gale I adore is not entirely a real person. The real Gale has become confused with my re-imagining of her, with my private elaboration of our continuing life together in an alternative universe devoid of ape-men. The real Gale may by now be beyond our grasp, ineffable.

I caught a glimpse of her recently. She was at the far end of a long, dark, subterranean bar-room guarded by freelance commandos bearing battlefield nuclear weapons. There were Polynesian snacks on the counter and beers from the Pacific rim on tap: Kirin, Tsingtao, Swan.

At that time many television channels were devoted to the sad case of the astronaut stranded on Mars without hope of rescue, and with diminishing supplies of food and breathable air. Official spokesmen told us of the persuasive arguments for the abrupt cancellation of the space exploration budget. We found these arguments powerful; influential voices complained of the sentimentality of the images of the dying spaceman. Nevertheless, the cameras inside his marooned craft continued to send us poignant pictures of his slow descent into despair, his low-gravity, weight-reduced death.

I watched my cousin Gale as she watched the bar's TV. She did not see me watching her, did not know that she had become my chosen programme.

The condemned man on another planet – the condemned man *on TV* – began to sing a squawky medley of half-remembered songs. I was reminded of the dying computer, Hal, in the old film *2001: A Space Odyssey*. Hal sang 'Daisy, Daisy' as it was being unplugged.

The Martian – for he was now a permanent resident of that planet – offered us his spaced-out renditions of 'Swanee', 'Show Me the Way to Go Home' and several numbers from *The Wizard of Oz*; and Gale's shoulders began to shake. She was crying.

I did not go across to comfort her.

I first heard about the upcoming auction of the ruby slippers the very next morning, and resolved at once to buy them, whatever the cost. My plan was simple: I would offer the miracle-shoes to Gale in all humility. If she wished, I would say, she could use them to travel to Mars and bring the spaceman back to Earth.

Perhaps I might even click the heels together three times, and win back her heart by murmuring, in soft reminder of our wasted love, *There's no place like home.*

You laugh at my desperation. Ha! Go tell a drowning man not to clutch at straws. Go ask a dying astronaut not to sing. Come here and stand in my shoes. What was it the Cowardly Lion said? Put 'em up. Put 'em uuuuup. I'll fight you with one hand tied behind my back. I'll fight you with my eyes closed.

Scared, huh? Scared?

The Grand Saleroom of the Auctioneers is the beating heart of the earth. If you stand here for long enough all the wonders of the world will pass by. In the Grand Saleroom, in recent years, we have witnessed the auction of the Taj Mahal, the Statue of Liberty, the Alps, the Sphinx. We have assisted at the sale of wives and the purchase of husbands. State secrets have been sold here, openly, to the highest bidder. On one very special occasion, the Auctioneers presided over the sale, to an overheated and inter-denominational bunch of smouldering red demons, of a wide selection of human souls of all classes, qualities, ages, races and creeds.

Everything is for sale, and under the firm yet essentially benevolent supervision of the Auctioneers, their security dogs and SWAT teams, we engage in a battle of wits and wallets, a war of nerves.

There is a purity about our actions here, and also an aesthetically pleasing tension between the vast complexity of the life that turns up, packaged into lots, to go under the hammer, and the equally immense simplicity of our manner of dealing with this life.

We bid, the Auctioneers knock a lot down, we pass on.

All are equal before the justice of the gavels: the pavement artist and Michelangelo, the slave girl and the Queen.

This is the courtroom of demand.

They are bidding for the slippers now. As the price rises, so does my gorge. Panic clutches at me, pulling me down, drowning me. I think of Gale – sweet coz! – and fight back fear, and bid.

Once I was asked by the widower of a world-famous and much-loved pop singer to attend an auction of rock memorabilia on his behalf. He was the sole trustee of her estate, which was worth tens of millions. I treated him with respect.

'There's only one lot I want,' he said. 'Spend whatever you have to spend.'

It was an article of clothing, a pair of edible rice-paper panties in peppermint flavour, purchased long ago in a store on (I think this was the name) Rodeo Drive. My employer's late wife's stage act had included the public removal and consumption of several such pairs. More panties, in a variety of flavours – chocolate chip, knickerbocker glory, cassata – were hurled into the crowd. These, too, were gobbled up in the general excitement of the concert, the lucky recipients being too carried away to consider the future value of what they had caught. Undergarments that had actually been worn by the lady were therefore in short supply, and presently in great demand.

During that auction, bids came in across the video links with Tokyo, Los Angeles, Paris and Milan, bids so rapid and of such size that I lost my nerve. However, when I telephoned my employer to confess my failure he was quite unperturbed, interested only in the final price. I mentioned a five-figure sum, and he laughed. It was the first genuinely joyful laugh I had heard from him since the day his wife died.

'That's all right then,' he said. 'I've got three hundred thousand of those.'

———

CHRISTOPHER COLUMBUS
AND
QUEEN ISABELLA OF SPAIN
CONSUMMATE THEIR
RELATIONSHIP
(SANTA FÉ, AD 1492)

Columbus, a foreigner, follows Queen Isabella for an eternity without entirely giving up hope.

— *In what characteristic postures?*

Proud yet supplicant, the head held high but the knee bent. Fawning yet fearless; possessed of a certain saucy vulgarity, he gets away with it by virtue of his confidence-man's charm. However, as time passes, the ingratiating aspects of his stance are emphasised; the sea-dog raffishness wears a little thin. As do his shoes.

= *His hope. It is of what?*

Obvious answers first. He hopes for preferment. He wants to tie the Queen's favour to his helmet, like a knight in a romance. (He owns no helmet.) He has hopes of cash, and of three tall ships, *Niña Pinta Santa Maria*; of, in fourteen hundred and ninety-two, sailing across the ocean blue. But, on his first arrival at court, when the Queen herself asked him what he desired, he bowed over her olive hand and, with his lips a breath away from the great ring of her power, murmured a single, dangerous word.

'Consummation.'

— *These unspeakable foreigners! The nerve! 'Consummation', indeed! And then following in her footsteps, month after month, as if he stood a chance.*

His coarse epistles, his tuneless serenades beneath her casement windows, obliging her to have them closed, shutting out the cooling breeze. She had better things to do, a world to conquer & so forth, who did he think he was?

= *Foreigners can be dogged. And can also, on account of language difficulties, fail to take a hint. Then again, let us not forget, it is considered* de rigueur *to keep a few foreigners around. They lend the place a certain cosmopolitan tone. They are often poor and consequently willing to perform divers necessary but dirty jobs. They are, moreover, a warning against complacency, their existence in our midst reminding us that there are quarters in which (hard as it is to accept) we ourselves would be considered foreign, too.*

— *But to speak so to the Queen!*

= *Foreigners forget their place (having left it behind). Given time, they begin to think of themselves as our equals. It is an unavoidable hazard. They introduce into our austerities their Italianate blandishments. Nothing for it: turn a deaf ear, look the other way. They rarely mean real harm, and go too far only infrequently. The Queen, be assured, can look after herself.*

Columbus at Isabella's court is quickly burdened with the reputation of being a crazy man. His clothes are excessively colourful and he drinks, also, to excess. When Isabella wins a military victory she celebrates it with eleven days of psalms and the sonorous severities of priests. Columbus crashes about outside the cathedral, waving a wineskin. He is a one-man debauch.

— *See him, the drunkard, his huge, shaggy head filled with nonsenses! A fool with a glittering eye dreaming of a golden paradise beyond the Western Edge of Things.*

'Consummation.'

The Queen plays with Columbus.

At luncheon she promises him everything he wants; then cuts him dead later the same afternoon, looking through him as if he were a veil.

On his saint's day she summons him to her inmost boudoir, dismisses her girls, permits him to braid her hair and, for a moment, to fondle her breasts. Then she summons her guards. She banishes him to the stables and piggeries for forty days. He sits forlorn on horse-munched hay while his thoughts run on distant, fabled gold. He dreams of the Queen's perfumes but awakes, gagging, in a pigsty.

Toying with Columbus pleases the Queen.

And pleasing the Queen, he reminds himself, may help him to achieve his purpose. Pigs rootle by his feet. He grits his teeth.

'Pleasing the Queen is good.'

Columbus ponders:

Does she torment him merely for sport?

Or: because he is foreign, and she is unused to his ways and meanings.

Or: because her ring finger, still hot with the memory of his lips his breath, has been – how-you-say? – *touched*. Yes: tentacles of warmth spread backward from her fingers towards her heart. A turbulence has been aroused.

Or: because she is torn between the possibility of embracing his scheme with a lover's abandon, and the more conventional, and differently (maliciously) pleasurable option of destroying him by laughing, finally, after much foreplay, in his foolish, supplicant face.

Columbus consoles himself with possibilities. Not all possibilities are consoling, however.

She is an absolute monarch. (Her husband is an absolute zero: a blank, couldn't be colder. We will not speak further of him.) She is a woman whose ring is often kissed. It means nothing to her. She is no stranger to flatteries. She resists them effortlessly.

She is a tyrant, who numbers among her possessions a private menagerie of four hundred and nineteen fools, some grotesquely malformed, others as beauteous as the dawn. He, Columbus, is merely her four hundred and twentieth idiot. This, too, is a plausible scenario.

Either: she understands his dream of a world beyond the world's end, and is moved by it, so profoundly that it spooks her, and she turns first towards it, then away;

Or: she doesn't understand him at all, nor cares to understand.

'Take your pick.'

What's certain is that *he* doesn't understand *her*. Only the facts are plain. She is Isabella, all-conquering Queen. He is her invisible (though raucous, multi-coloured, wine-bibbing) man.

'Consummation.'

The sexual appetites of the male decline; those of the female continue, with the advancing years, to grow. Isabella is Columbus's last hope. He is running out of possible patrons, sales talk, flirtatiousness, hair, steam.

Time drags by.

Isabella gallops around, winning battles, expelling

Moors from their strongholds, her appetites expanding by the week. The more of the land she swallows, the more warriors she engulfs, the hungrier she gets. Columbus, aware of a slow shrivelling inside him, scolds himself. He should see things as they are. He should come to his senses. What chance does he have here? Some days she makes him clean latrines. On other days he is on body-washing duty, and after a battle the bodies are not clean. Soldiers going to war wear man-sized diapers under their armour because the fear of death will open the bowels, will do it every time. Columbus was not cut out for this sort of work. He tells himself to leave Isabella, once and for all.

But there are problems: his advancing years, the patron shortage. Once he decamps, he will have to forget the western voyage.

The body of philosophical opinion which holds that life is absurd has never appealed to him. He is a man of action, revealing himself in deeds. But without the western voyage he will be obliged to accept the meaninglessness of life. This, too, would be a defeat. Invisible in hot tropical colours, unrequited, he remains, dogging her footsteps, hoping for the ecstasy of her glance.

'The search for money and patronage', Columbus says, 'is not so different from the quest for love.'

———

—   *She is omnipotent. Castles fall at her feet. The Jews have been expelled. The Moors prepare their last surrender. The Queen is at Granada, riding at her armies' head.*

=   *She overwhelms. Nothing she has wanted has ever been refused.*

—   *All her dreams are prophecies.*

=   *Acting upon information received while sleeping, she draws up her invincible battle plans, foils the conspiracies of assassins, learns of the infidelities and corruptions for which she blackmails both her loyalists (to ensure their support) and her opponents (to ensure theirs). The dreams help her forecast the weather, negotiate treaties, and invest shrewdly in trade.*

—   *She eats like a horse and never gains an ounce.*

=   *The earth adores her footfall. Its shadows flee before the brilliance of her eyes.*

—   *Her face is a lush peninsula set in a sea of hair.*

=   *Her treasure chests are inexhaustible.*

—   *Her ears are soft question-marks, suggesting some uncertainty.*

=   *Her legs.*

—   *Her legs are not so great.*

= *She is full of discontents.*

— *No conquest satisfies her, no peak of ecstasy is high enough.*

= *See: there at the gates of the Alhambra is Boabdil the Unlucky, the last Sultan of the last redoubt of all the centuries of Arab Spain. Behold: now, at this very instant, he surrenders the keys to the citadel into her grasp . . . there! And as the weight of the keys falls from his hand into hers, she . . . she . . .* yawns.

Columbus gives up hope.

While Isabella is entering the Alhambra in listless triumph, he is saddling his mule. While she dawdles in the Court of the Lions, he departs in a flurry of whips elbows hooves, all rapidly obscured by a dust cloud.

Invisibility claims him. He surrenders to its will. Knowing he is abandoning his destiny, he abandons it. He rides away from Queen Isabella in hopeless anger, rides day and night, and when his mule dies under him he shoulders his ridiculous gypsy-patchwork bags, their rowdy colours muted now by dirt; and walks.

Around him stretches the rich plain her armies have subdued. Columbus sees none of it, neither the land's fertility nor the sudden barrenness of the vanquished castles looking down from their pinnacles. The ghosts of defeated civilisations flow unnoticed down the rivers whose names – Guadalthis and Guadalthat – retain an echo of the annihilated past.

Overhead, the arabesque wheelings of the patient buzzards.

Jews pass Columbus in long columns, but the tragedy of their expulsion makes no mark on him. Somebody tries to sell him a Toledo sword; he waves the man away. Having lost his own dream of ships, Columbus leaves the Jews to the ships of their exile, waiting in the harbour of Cadiz. Exhaustion strips him of his senses. This old world is too old and the new world is an unfound land.

'The loss of money and patronage', Columbus says, 'is as bitter as unrequited love.'

He walks beyond fatigue, beyond the limits of endurance and the frontiers of self, and somewhere along this path he loses his balance, he falls off the edge of his sanity, and out here beyond his mind's rim he sees, for the first and only time in his life, a vision.

It is a dream of a dream.

He dreams of Isabella, languidly exploring the Alhambra, the great jewel she has seized from Boabdil, last of the Nasrids.

She is staring into a large stone bowl held aloft by stone lions. The bowl is filled with blood, and in it she sees – *that is, Columbus dreams her seeing* – a vision of her own.

The bowl shows her that everything, all the known world, is now hers. Everyone in it is in her hands, to do with as she pleases. And when she understands this – *Columbus dreams* – the blood at once congeals, becoming a thick and verminous sludge. Whereupon the Isabella of Columbus's weary, but also vengeful, imaginings is shaken to her very marrow by the realisation that she will never, *never*, NEVER! be satisfied by the possession of the Known. Only the Unknown, perhaps even the Unknowable, can satisfy her.

All at once she remembers Columbus (*he envisions her remembering him*). Columbus, the invisible man who dreams of entering the invisible world, the unknown and perhaps even unknowable world beyond the Edge of Things, beyond the stone bowl of the everyday, beyond the thick blood of the sea. Columbus in this bitter dream makes Isabella see the truth at last, makes her accept that her need for him is as great as his for her. Yes! She knows it now! She must must must give him the money, the ships, anything, and he must must must carry her flag and her favour beyond the end of the end of the earth, into exaltation and immortality, linking her to him for ever with bonds far harder to dissolve than those of any mortal love, the harsh and deifying ties of history.

'Consummation.'

In Columbus's savage dream, Isabella tears her hair, runs from the Court of the Lions, screams for her heralds.

'Find him,' she commands.

But Columbus in his dream refuses to be found. He wraps around himself the dusty patchwork cloak of his invisibility, and the heralds gallop hither and yon in vain.

Isabella screeches, beseeches, implores.

Bitch! Bitch! How do you like it now, Columbus sneers. By absenting himself from her court, by this final and suicidal invisibility, he has denied her her heart's desire. Serves her right.

Bitch!

She murdered his hopes, didn't she? Well, then. In doing so she has laid herself low as well. Poetic justice. Fair's fair.

———

At the dream's end he permits her messengers to find him. Their hoofbeats, their waving frantic arms. They plead, cajole, offer bribes. But it's too late. Only the sweet self-lacerating joy of murdering Possibility remains.

He answers the heralds: a shake of the head.

'No.'

He comes to his senses.

He is on his knees in the fertility of the plains, waiting for death. He hears the hoofbeats approaching and raises his eyes, half expecting to see the Exterminating Angel, riding towards him like a conqueror. Its black wings, the boredom on its face.

Isabella's heralds surround him. They offer him food, drink, a horse. They are shouting.

— *Good news! The Queen has summoned you.*

= *Your voyage: wonderful news.*

— *She saw a vision, and it scared her.*

= *All her dreams are prophecies.*

The heralds dismount. They offer bribes, plead, cajole.

— *She ran from the Court of the Lions, shouting out your name.*

= *She will send you beyond the stone bowl of the known world, beyond the thick blood of the sea.*

EAST, WEST

THE HARMONY OF
THE SPHERES

In the time of the Jubilee the writer Eliot Crane, who had been suffering from what he called 'brainstorms' of paranoid schizophrenia, had lunch with his wife, a young photo-journalist called Lucy Evans, in the Welsh town of R., where she was working on the local paper. He looked cheerful, and told her he was feeling fine, but tired, and would go to bed early. It was the paper's press night, so Lucy was late getting home to their hillside cottage; when she went upstairs Eliot wasn't in their bedroom. Assuming that he was sleeping in the spare room, so that she wouldn't disturb him, she went to bed.

An hour later Lucy woke up with a premonition of disaster and went without getting dressed to the door of the guest bedroom; which, taking a deep breath, she opened. Half a second later, she slammed it shut again, and slumped heavily to the floor. He had been ill for more than two years, and all she could think was *It's over.* When she started shivering she went back to bed and slept soundly until morning.

He had sucked on his shotgun and pulled the trigger. The weapon had belonged to his father, who had put it to the same use. The only suicide note Eliot left after perpetrating this final act of macabre symmetry was a meticulous account of how to clean and care for the gun. He and Lucy had no children. He was thirty-two years old.

A week earlier, the three of us walked up a beacon hill in the Borders to see the Jubilee bonfires flowering along the spine of the country, garlanding the darkness. 'It doesn't mean a "good fire",' Eliot said, 'though I grant there's an element of that in the word. Originally it was a fire made of bones: the bones of dead animals but also, fee fi fo fum, human remains, the charred skeletons my dears of *yuman beans*.'

He had wild red hair and a laugh like an owl's hoot and was as thin as a witch's stick. In the firelight's bright shadow-theatre we all looked insane, so it was easier to discount his hollowed-out cheeks, the pantomime cockings of his eyebrows, the mad-sailor glitter in his eye. We stood close to the flames and Eliot told dread tales of local Sabbats, at which cloaked and urine-drinking sorcerers conjured devils up from Hell. We swigged brandy from his silver hip-flask and recoiled on cue. But he had met a demon once and ever since that day he and Lucy had been on the run. They had sold their haunted home, a tiny house in Portugal Place, Cambridge, and moved to the bleak, sheep-smelly Welsh cottage they named (with gallows humour) Crowley End.

It hadn't worked. As we shrieked at Eliot's ghost stories, we knew that the demon had traced the number on his car licence-plates, that it could call him any time on his unlisted telephone; that it had rediscovered his home address.

'You'd better come,' Lucy had called to say. 'They found him going the wrong way on the motorway, doing ninety, with one of those sleep-mask things over his eyes.' She had given up a lot for him, quitting her job on a London Sunday paper and settling for a hicksville gazette, because he was mad, and she needed to be close.

'Am I approved of at present?' I'd asked. Eliot had elaborated a conspiracy theory in which most of his friends were revealed to be agents of hostile powers, both Earthly and extra-terrestrial. I was an invader from Mars, one of many such dangerous beings who had sneaked into Britain when certain essential forms of vigilance had been relaxed. Martians had great gifts of mimicry, so they could fool yuman beans into believing they were beans of the same stripe, and of course they bred like fruit-flies on a pile of rotten bananas.

For more than a year, during my Martian phase, I had been unable to visit. Lucy would phone with bulletins: the drugs were working, the drugs were not working because he refused to take them regularly, he seemed better as long as he did not try to write, he seemed worse because not writing plunged him into such deep depressions, he was passive and inert, he was raging and violent, he was filled with guilt and despair.

I felt helpless; as one does.

We became friends in my last year at Cambridge, while I was involved in an exhausting on-off love affair with a graduate student named Laura. Her thesis was on James Joyce and the French *nouveau roman*, and to please her I ploughed my way through *Finnegans Wake* twice, and most of Sarraute, Butor and Robbe-Grillet too. One night, seized by romance, I climbed out of the window of her flat in Chesterton Road, balanced precariously on the window-sill and refused to come back inside until she agreed to marry me. The next morning she rang her mother to break the news. After a long silence, Mummy said, 'I'm sure he's very nice, dear, but couldn't you find someone of, you know, your own kind?'

Laura was humiliated by the question. 'What do you mean, my own kind?' she yelled down the phone. 'A Joyce specialist? A person five feet and three inches tall? A woman?'

That summer, however, she got stoned at a wedding,

ten years I recognised at once that we had kissed on the beach at Juhu when I was fourteen and she was twelve; and that I was anxious to repeat the experience. Miss Lucy Evans, the honey-blonde, precocious daughter of the boss of the famous Bombay Company. She made no mention of kisses; I thought she had probably forgotten them, and said nothing either. But then she reminisced about our camel-races on Juhu beach, and fresh coconut-milk, straight from the tree. She hadn't forgotten.

Lucy was the proud owner of a small cabin cruiser, an ancient craft that had once been a naval longboat. It was pointed at both ends, had a makeshift cabin in the middle and a Thorneycroft Handybilly engine of improbable antiquity which would respond to nobody's coaxings except hers. It had been to Dunkirk. She named it *Bougainvillaea* in memory of her child-hood in Bombay.

I joined Eliot and Lucy aboard *Bougainvillaea* several times, the first time with Mala, but subsequently without her. Mala, now Doctor Mala, Doctor (Mrs) Khan, no less, the Mona Lisa of the Harrow Road Medical Centre, was repelled by that bohemian exist-ence in which we did without baths and pissed over the side and huddled together for warmth at night, zipped into our quilted sacks. 'For me, hygiene-comfort are

Priority A,' said Mala. 'Let sleeping bags lie. I-tho will stay home with my Dunlopillo and WC.'

There was a trip we took up the Trent and Mersey Canal as far as Middlewich, then west to Nantwich, south down the Shropshire Union Canal, and west again to Llangollen. Lucy as skipper was intensely desirable, revealing great physical strength and a kind of boaty bossiness that I found very arousing. On this trip we had two nights alone, because Eliot had to return to Cambridge to hear a lecture by a 'top man from Austria' on the subject of the Nazis and the occult. We saw him off at Crewe station and then ate a bad meal in a restaurant with pretensions. Lucy insisted on ordering a bottle of rosé wine. The waitress stiffened contemptuously. 'The French for red, madam,' she bellowed, 'is *rouge*.'

Whatever it was, we drank too much of it. Later, aboard *Bougainvillaea*, we zipped our sleeping bags together and returned to Juhu beach. But at a certain moment she kissed my cheek, murmured 'Madness, love', and rolled over, turning her back on the too-distant past. I thought of Mala, my not-too-distant present, and blushed guiltily in the dark.

———

The next day, neither of us spoke of what had almost happened. *Bougainvillaea* arrived at a one-way tunnel at the wrong time; but Lucy didn't feel like waiting three hours for her right of way. She ordered me to go ahead with a torch along the narrow towpath inside the tunnel, while she brought the boat on behind me at a crawl. I had no idea what she'd do if we met anyone coming towards us, but my journey along the slippery, broken towpath required all my attention, and anyway, I was only the crew.

Our luck held; we emerged into the daylight. I had been wearing a white cricket sweater which was now bright red, stained indelibly by mud from the tunnel walls. There was mud in my shoes and in my hair and on my face. When I wiped my sweating forehead a lump of mud fell into my eye.

Lucy whooped in triumph at our illegal success. 'Made a lawbreaker of you at last, bloody wonderful,' she hollered. (As a youth, in Bombay, I had been notoriously Good.) 'You see? Crime does pay, after all.'

Madness. Love. I remembered the rosé and the tunnel when I heard about Eliot's high-speed escapade. Our adventures aboard *Bougainvillaea* by night and by day had been as dangerous, in their way. Forbidden embraces and a wrong-way journey in the dark. But we weren't shipwrecked, and he wasn't killed. Just lucky. I suppose.

Why do we lose our minds?

'A simple biochemical imbalance,' was Eliot's view. He insisted on driving home from the Jubilee bonfire, and as he accelerated through blind corners on lightless country roads, various biochemicals surged, off-balance, through my veins as well. Then, without warning, he braked hard and stopped. It was a clear night with a moon. On the hillside to our right were sleeping sheep and a small fenced-off graveyard.

'I want to be buried here,' he announced.

'No can do,' I answered from the back seat. 'You'd have to be dead, you see.'

'Don't,' said Lucy. 'You'll only give him ideas.'

We were teasing him to conceal the quaking within, but Eliot knew we had registered the information. He nodded, satisfied; and accelerated.

'If you wipe us out,' I gasped, 'who'll be left to remember you when you're gone?'

When we got back to Crowley End he went straight to bed without a word. Lucy looked in on him a while later and reported that he'd fallen asleep fully clothed, and grinning. 'Let's get drunk,' she suggested brightly.

She stretched out on the floor in front of the fire.

But in the case of Eliot and me, I do know, really. It was that old black magic. Not love, not chocolate: the Hidden Arts. If I find it impossible to let go of Eliot's memory, it is perhaps because I know that the seductive arcana which drove Eliot Crane out of his mind almost ensnared me as well.

Pentangles, illuminati, Maharishi, Gandalf: necromancy was part of the *zeitgeist*, of the private language of the counter-culture. From Eliot I learned the secrets of the Great Pyramid, the mysteries of the Golden Section and the intricacies of the Spiral. He told me about Mesmer's theory of Animal Magnetism (*A responsive influence exists between the heavenly bodies, the earth and all animated bodies. A fluid universally diffused, incomparably subtle, is the means of this influence. It is subject to mechanical laws with which we are not yet familiar*) and the Four Trances of Japanese spiritualism: *Muchu*, that is, ecstasy or rapture; *Shissi, Konsui-Jotai*, or a coma; *Saimin-Jotai*, a hypnotic state; and *Mugen no Kyo*, in which the soul can leave the body behind and wander in the World of Mystery. Through Eliot I met remarkable men, or at least their minds: G.I. Gurdjieff, author of *Beelzebub's Tales* and guru to, among others, Aldous Huxley, Katherine Mansfield and J.B. Priestley; and Raja Rammohun Roy and his

Brahmo Samaj, that brave attempt at making a synthesis of Indian and English thought.

Under my friend's informal tutelage, I studied numerology and palmistry and memorised an Indian spell for flying. I was taught the verses that conjured up the Devil, *Shaitan*, and how to draw the shape that would keep the Beast 666 confined.

I never had much time for gurus back home where the word came from, but that's what Eliot was, I confess with a blush. A mystical teacher in English translation; say it g'*roo*.

Reader: I flunked the course. I never experienced *Muchu* (much less *Mugen no Kyo*), never dared speak the Hell-raising spells, or jumped off a cliff, like some Yaquí *brujo*'s apprentice, to fly.

I survived.

Eliot and I practised putting each other under hypnosis. Once he implanted the post-hypnotic suggestion that if he should ever say the word 'bananas' I must at once remove all my clothes. That evening, on the dance-floor at Dingwall's club with Mala and Lucy, he whispered his fruity malice into my ear. Rumbling, sleep-inducing waves began to roll heavily over me and even though I tried hard to fight them back my hands began to undress me. When they began unzipping my jeans we were all thrown out.

'You boys,' Mala said disapprovingly as I dressed by the canal, swearing loudly and threatening dire revenges. 'Maybe you should go to bed together and we-all can go home and get some rest.'

Was that it? No. Maybe. No. I don't know. *No.*

What a picture: a double portrait of self-deceivers. Eliot the occultist pretending to be an academic, with me, more prosaically, perhaps, half-lost in occult love.

Was that it?

When I met Eliot I was a little unhinged myself – suffering from a disharmony of my personal spheres. There was the Laura episode, and beyond it a number of difficult questions about home and identity that I had no idea how to answer. Eliot's instinct about Mala and me was one answer that I was grateful for. Home, like Hell, turned out to be other people. For me, it turned out to be her.

Not Martian, but Mauritian. She was a ninth-generation child of indentured labourers brought from India after the black exodus that had followed the end of slavery. At home – home was a small village to the north of Port Louis, and its largest edifice was a small white Vishnu temple – she and her family had spoken a version of the Indian Bhojpuri dialect, so creolised over the years as to be virtually incomprehensible to non-Mauritian Indians. She had never been to India, and my birth and childhood and continued connections there made me, in her eyes, ridiculously glamorous, like a visitor from Xanadu. *For he on honey-dew hath fed, And drunk the milk of Paradise.*

Even though she was, as she put it, 'from science side', she was interested in writing, and liked the fact that I was trying to be a writer. She took pride in 'Romeo and Juliet of Mauritius', as she called Bernardin de St Pierre's *Paul et Virginie*; and insisted that I read it. 'Maybe it will influence,' she said, hopefully.

She had a doctor's unsqueamishness and practicality, and like all people 'from arts side' I envied her knowledge of what human beings were like on the inside. What I had to imagine about human nature, she gave every appearance of knowing. She wasn't a big talker, but I felt that in her I had found my rock. And the warm dark tides of the Indian Ocean rose nightly in her veins.

What angered her, it seemed, was Eliot, and my closeness to him. Once she was installed as my wife – we honeymooned in Venice – her unease prompted what was, for her, a major speech. 'All that mumboing and jumboing,' she snorted, full of science-side contempt for the Irrational. 'So phoney, God! Listen: he comes round too much, it's bad for you. What is he? Some English mess-head, only. Get my drift, writer sahib? I mean, thanks for the intro etcetera, but now you should drop him, like a brick.'

'Welsh,' I said, very surprised. 'He's Welsh.'

'Doesn't matter,' snapped Doctor (Mrs) Khan. 'Diagnosis still applies.'

But in Eliot's enormous, generously shared mental storehouse of the varieties of 'forbidden knowledge' I thought I'd found another way of making a bridge between here-and-there, between my two othernesses, my double unbelonging. In that world of magic and power there seemed to exist the kind of fusion of world-views, European Amerindian Oriental Levantine, in which I desperately wanted to believe.

With his help, I hoped, I might make a 'forbidden self'. The apparent world, all cynicism and napalm, seemed wholly without kindness or wisdom. The hidden realm, in which Sufis walked with Adepts and great secrets could be glimpsed, would show me how to be wise. It would grant me – Eliot's favourite word, this – harmony.

Mala was right. He couldn't help anyone, the poor sap; couldn't even save himself. In the end his demons came for him, his Gurdjieff and Ouspensky and his Crowley and Blavatsky, his Dunsany and his Lovecraft long ago. They crowded out the sheep on his Welsh hillside, and closed in on his mind.

Harmony? You never heard such a din as the ruckus in Eliot's head. The songs of Swedenborg's angels, the hymns, the mantras, the Tibetan overtone chants. What human mind could have defended itself against such a Babel, in which Theosophists argued with Confucians, Christian Scientists with Rosicrucians? Here were devotees praising the coming of Lord Maitreya; there, blood-sucking wizards hurling curses. And lo, there came forth Millenarians crying Doom; and behold, Hitler arose brandishing his fylfot, which in his ignorance or malignity he gave the name of the symbol of good: *swastika*.

In the throng besieging the sick man of Crowley End even my personal favourite, Raja Rammohun Roy, was just another voice in the cacodemonic crowd.

Bang!

And, at last, silence. *Requiescat in pace.*

By the time I got back to Wales, Lucy's brother Bill had called the police and undertakers and had spent heroic hours in the spare room cleaning the blood and brains off the walls. Lucy sat sipping gin in the kitchen in a light summer frock, looking dreadfully composed.

'Would you go through his books and papers?' she asked me, sounding sweet and distant. 'I can't do it. There may be enough of the Glendower thing. Someone could pull it into shape.'

It took me the best part of a week, that sad excavation of my dead friend's unpublished mind. I felt a page turning; I was just starting to be a writer then, and Eliot had just stopped being one. Although in truth, as I found, he had stopped being one years ago. There was no trace of a Glendower manuscript, or any serious work at all. There were only ravings.

Bill Evans had stuffed three tea-chests with Eliot's typed and scribbled papers. In these chests of delirium I found hundreds of pages of operatic, undirected obscenities and inchoate rants against the universe in general. There were dozens of notebooks in which Eliot had dreamed up alternative personal futures of extraordinary distinction and renown, or, alternatively, self-pitying versions of a life of genius-in-obscurity ending in agonising illnesses, or assassination by jealous rivals; after which, inevitably, came recognition by a remorseful world of the greatness it had ignored. These were sorry reams.

Harder still to read were his fantasies about us, his friends. These were of two kinds: hate-filled, and pornographic. There were many virulent attacks on me, and pages of steamy sex involving my wife Mala, 'dated', no doubt to maximise their auto-erotic effect, in the days immediately after our marriage. And, of course, at other times. The pages about Lucy were both nasty and lubricious. I searched the tea-chests in vain for a loving remark. It was hard to believe that such a passionate and eager man could have nothing good to say about life on earth. Yet it was so.

I showed Lucy nothing, but she saw it all on my face. 'It wasn't really him writing,' she consoled me mechanically. 'He was sick.'

And I know what made him sick, I thought; and vowed silently to remain well. Since then there has been no intercourse between the spiritual world and mine. Mesmer's 'influential fluid' evaporated for ever as I plunged through the putrid tea-chests of my friend's mad filth.

Eliot was buried according to his wishes. The manner of his dying had created some difficulties regarding the use of consecrated ground, but Lucy's fury had persuaded the local clergy to turn a blind eye.

Among the mourners was a Conservative Member

of Parliament who had been at school with Eliot. 'Poor Elly,' this man said in a loud voice. 'We used to ask ourselves, "*Whatever will become of Elly Crane?*" And I'd say, "*He'll probably make something half-way decent of his life, if he doesn't kill himself first.*" '

This gentleman is presently a member of the Cabinet, and receives Special Branch protection. I don't think he realises how close he came to needing protection (against me) on a sunny morning in Wales long ago.

But his epitaph is the only one I remember.

At the moment of our parting Lucy gave me her hand to shake. We didn't see each other again. I heard that she had remarried quickly and dully and gone to live in the American West.

Back home, I found that I needed to talk for a long time. Mala sat and listened sympathetically. Eventually I told her about the tea-chests.

'You worked him out, no need to remind me,' I cried. 'You knew his insides. Imagine! He was so sick, so crazy, that he fantasised all these frenzied last-tango encounters with you. For instance, just after we got home from Venice. For instance, in those two days I was alone with Lucy on *Bougainvillaea*, and he said he had to go to Cambridge for a lecture.'

Mala stood up and turned her back on me, and

before she spoke I guessed her answer, feeling it explode in my chest with an unbearable raucous crack, a sound reminiscent of the break-up of log-jams or pack-ice. Yes, she had warned me against Eliot Crane, warned me with the bitter passion of her denunciation of him; and I, in my surprise at the denunciation, had failed to hear the real warning, failed to understand what she had meant by the passion in her voice. *That mess-head. He's bad for you.*

So, here it came: the collapse of harmony, the demolition of the spheres of my heart.

'Those weren't fantasies,' she said.

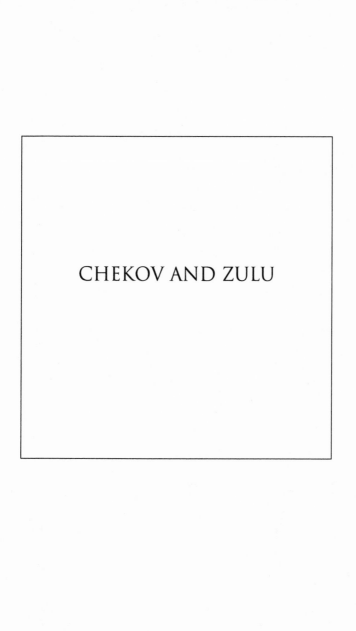

CHEKOV AND ZULU

I

On 4th November, 1984, Zulu disappeared in Birmingham, and India House sent his old schoolfriend Chekov to Wembley to see the wife.

'Adaabarz, Mrs Zulu. Permission to enter?'

'Of course come in, Dipty sahib, why such formality?'

'Sorry to disturb you on a Sunday, Mrs Zulu, but Zulu-tho hasn't been in touch this morning?'

'With me? Since when he contacts me on official trip? Why to hit a telephone call when he is probably enjoying?'

'Whoops, sore point, excuse *me*. Always been the foot-in-it blunderbuss type.'

'At least sit, take tea-shee.'

'Fixed the place up damn fine, Mrs Zulu, wah-wah. Tasteful decor, in spades, I must say. So much cut-glass! That bounder Zulu must be getting too much pay, more than yours truly, clever dog.'

'No, how is it possible? Acting Dipty's tankha must be far in excess of Security Chief.'

'No suspicion intended, ji. Only to say what a bargain-hunter you must be.'

'Some problem but there is, na?'

'Beg pardon?'

'Arré, Jaisingh! Where have you been sleeping? Acting Dipty Sahib is thirsting for his tea. And biscuits and jalebis, can you not keep two things in your head? Jump, now, guest is waiting.'

'Truly, Mrs Zulu, please go to no trouble.'

'No trouble is there, Diptyji, only this chap has become lazy since coming from home. Days off, TV in room, even pay in pounds sterling, he expects all. So far we brought him but no gratitude, what to tell you, noth-*thing*.'

'Ah, Jaisingh; why not? Excellent jalebi, Mrs Z. Thanking you.'

Assembled on top of the television and on shelf units around it was the missing man's collection of *Star Trek* memorabilia: Captain Kirk and Spock dolls, spaceship models – a Klingon Bird of Prey, a Romulan vessel, a space station, and of course the Starship *Enterprise*. In pride of place were large figurines of two of the series's supporting cast.

'These old Doon School nicknames,' Chekov exclaimed heartily. 'They stay put like stuck records. Dumpy, Stumpy, Grumpy, Humpy. They take over from our names. As in our case our intrepid cosmonaut aliases.'

'I don't like. This "Mrs Zulu" I am landed with! It sounds like a blackie.'

'Wear the name with pride, begum sahib. We're old comrades-in-arms, your husband and I; since boyhood days, perhaps he was good enough to mention? Intrepid diplonauts. Our umpteen-year mission to explore new worlds and new civilisations. See there, our alter egos standing on your TV, the Asiatic-looking Russky and the Chink. Not the leaders, as you'll appreciate, but the ultimate professional servants. "Course laid in!" "Hailing frequencies open!" "Warp factor three!" What would that strutting Captain have been without his top-level staffers? Likewise with the good ship Hindustan. We are servants also, you see, just like your fierce Jaisingh here. Never more important than in a moment like the present sad crisis, when an even keel must be maintained, jalebis must be served and tea poured, no matter what. We do not lead, but we enable. Without us, no course can be laid, no hailing frequency opened. No factors can be warped.'

'Is he in difficulties, then, your Zulu? As if it wasn't bad enough, this terrible time.'

On the wall behind the TV was a framed photograph of Indira Gandhi, with a garland hung around it. She had been dead since Wednesday. Pictures of her cremation had been on the TV for hours. The flower-petals, the garish, unbearable flames.

'Hard to believe it. Indiraji! Words fail one. She was our mother. Hai, hai! Cut down in her prime.'

'And on radio-TV, such-such stories are coming about Delhi goings-on. So many killings, Dipty Sahib. So many of our decent Sikh people done to death, as if all were guilty for the crimes of one-two badmash guards.'

'The Sikh community has always been thought loyal to the nation,' Chekov reflected. 'Backbone of the Army, to say nothing of the Delhi taxi service. Super-citizens, one might say, seemingly wedded to the national idea. But such ideas are being questioned now, you must admit; there are those who would point to the comb, bangle, dagger et cetera as signs of the enemy within.'

'Who would dare say such a thing about us? Such an evil thing.'

'I know. I know. But you take Zulu. The ticklish thing is, he's not on any official business that we know of. He's dropped off the map, begum sahib. AWOL ever since the assassination. No contact for two days plus.'

'O God.'

'There is a view forming back at HQ that he may have been associated with the gang. Who have in all probability long-established links with the community over here.'

'O God.'

'Naturally I am fighting strenuously against the proponents of this view. But his absence is damning, you must see. We have no fear of these tinpot Khalistan wallahs. But they have a ruthless streak. And with Zulu's inside knowledge and security background . . . They have threatened further attacks, as you know. As you must know. As some would say you must know all too well.'

'O God.'

'It is possible', Chekov said, eating his jalebi, 'that Zulu has boldly gone where no Indian diplonaut has gone before.'

The wife wept. 'Even the stupid name you could never get right. It was with S. "Sulu." So-so many episodes I have been made to see, you think I don't know? Kirk Spock McCoy Scott Uhura Chekov *Sulu*.'

'But Zulu is a better name for what some might allege to be a wild man,' Chekov said. 'For a suspected savage. For a putative traitor. Thank you for excellent tea.'

2

In August, Zulu, a shy, burly giant, had met Chekov off the plane from Delhi. Chekov at thirty-three was a small, slim, dapper man in grey flannels, stiff-collared shirt and a double-breasted navy blue blazer with brass buttons. He had bat's-wing eyebrows and a prominent and pugnacious jaw, so that his cultivated tones and habitual soft-spokenness came as something of a surprise, disarming those who had been led by the eyebrows and chin to expect an altogether more aggressive personality. He was a high flyer, with one small embassy already notched up. The Acting Number Two job in London, while strictly temporary, was his latest plum.

'What-ho, Zools! Years, yaar, years,' Chekov said, thumping his palm into the other man's chest. 'So,' he added, 'I see you've become a hairy fairy.' The young Zulu had been a modern Sikh in the matter of hair – sporting a fine moustache at eighteen, but beardless, with a haircut instead of long tresses wound tightly under a turban. Now, however, he had reverted to tradition.

'Hullo, ji,' Zulu greeted him cautiously. 'So then is it OK to utilise the old modes of address?'

'Utilise away! Wouldn't hear of anything else,' Chekov said, handing Zulu his bags and baggage tags. 'Spirit of the *Enterprise* and all that jazz.'

In his public life the most urbane of men, Chekov when letting his hair down in private enjoyed getting interculturally hot under the collar. Soon after his taking up his new post he sat with Zulu one lunchtime on a bench in Embankment Gardens and jerked his head in the direction of various passers-by.

'Crooks,' he said, *sotto voce*.

'Where?' shouted Zulu, leaping athletically to his feet. 'Should I pursue?'

Heads turned. Chekov grabbed the hem of Zulu's jacket and pulled him back on to the bench. 'Don't be such a hero,' he admonished fondly. 'I meant all of them, generally; thieves, every last one. God, I love London! Theatre, ballet, opera, restaurants! The Pavilion at Lord's on the Saturday of the Test Match! The royal ducks on the royal pond in royal St James's Park! Decent tailors, a decent mixed grill when you want it, decent magazines to read! I see the remnants of greatness and I don't mind telling you I am impressed. The Athenaeum, Buck House, the lions in Trafalgar Square. *Damn* impressive. I went to a meeting with the junior Minister at the F. & C.O. and realised I was in the old India Office. All that John Company black teak, those tuskers rampant on the old bookcases. Gave me quite a turn. I applaud them for their success: hurrah! But then I look at my own home, and I see that it has been plundered by burglars. I can't deny there is a residue of distress.'

'I am sorry to hear of your loss,' Zulu said, knitting his brows. 'But surely the culpables are not in the vicinity.'

'Zulu, Zulu, a figure of speech, my simpleton warrior prince. Their museums are full of our treasures, I meant. Their fortunes and cities, built on the loot they took. So on, so forth. One forgives, of course; that is our national nature. One need not forget.'

Zulu pointed at a tramp, sleeping on the next bench in a ragged hat and coat. 'Did he steal from us, too?' he asked.

'Never forget', said Chekov, wagging a finger, 'that the British working class collaborated for its own gain in the colonial project. Manchester cotton workers, for instance, supported the destruction of our cotton industry. As diplomats we must never draw attention to such facts; but facts, nevertheless, they remain.'

'But a beggarman is not in the working class,' objected Zulu, reasonably. 'Surely this fellow at least is not our oppressor.'

'Zulu,' Chekov said in exasperation, 'don't be so bleddy difficult.'

Chekov and Zulu went boating on the Serpentine, and Chekov got back on his hobby-horse. 'They have stolen us,' he said, reclining boatered and champagned on striped cushions while mighty Zulu rowed. 'And now we are stealing ourselves back. It is an Elgin marbles situation.'

'You should be more content,' said Zulu, shipping oars and gulping cola. 'You should be less hungry, less cross. See how much you have! It is enough. Sit back and enjoy. I have less, and it suffices for me. The sun is shining. The colonial period is a closed book.'

'If you don't want that sandwich, hand it over,' said Chekov. 'With my natural radicalism I should not have been a diplomat. I should have been a terrorist.'

'But then we would have been enemies, on opposite sides,' protested Zulu, and suddenly there were real tears in his eyes. 'Do you care nothing for our friendship? For my responsibilities in life?'

Chekov was abashed. 'Quite right, Zools old boy. Too bleddy true. You can't imagine how delighted I was when I learned we would be able to join forces like this in London. Nothing like the friendships of one's boyhood, eh? Nothing in the world can take their place. Now listen, you great lummox, no more of that long face. I won't permit it. Great big chap like you shouldn't look like he's about to blub. Blood brothers, old friend, what do you say? All for one and one for all.'

'Blood brothers,' said Zulu, smiling a shy smile.

'Onward, then,' nodded Chekov, settling back on his cushions. 'Impulse power only.'

———

The day Mrs Gandhi was murdered by her Sikh body-guards, Zulu and Chekov played squash in a private court in St John's Wood. In the locker-room after showering, prematurely-greying Chekov still panted heavily with a towel round his softening waist, reluctant to expose his exhaustion-shrivelled purple penis to view; Zulu stood proudly naked, thick-cocked, tossing his fine head of long black hair, caressing and combing it with womanly sensuality, and at last twisting it swiftly into a knot.

'Too good, Zulu yaar. Fataakh! Fataakh! What shots! Too bleddy good for me.'

'You desk-pilots, ji. You lose your edge. Once you were ready for anything.'

'Yeah, yeah, I'm over the hill. But you were only one year junior.'

'I have led a purer life, ji – action, not words.'

'You understand we will have to blacken your name,' Chekov said softly.

Zulu turned slowly in Charles Atlas pose in front of a full-length mirror.

'It has to look like a maverick stunt. If anything goes wrong, deniability is essential. Even your wife must not suspect the truth.'

Spreading his arms and legs, Zulu made his body a

giant X, stretching himself to the limit. Then he came to attention. Chekov sounded a little frayed.

'Zools? What do you say?'

'Is the transporter ready?'

'Come on, yaar, don't arse around.'

'Respectfully, Mister Chekov, sir, it's my arse. Now then: is the transporter ready?'

'Transporter ready. Aye.'

'Then, energise.'

Chekov's memorandum, classified top-secret, eyes-only, and addressed to 'JTK' (James T. Kirk):

My strong recommendation is that Operation Star-trek be aborted. To send a Federation employee of Klingon origin unarmed into a Klingon cell to spy is the crudest form of loyalty test. The operative in question has never shown ideological deviation of any sort and deserves better, even in the present climate of mayhem, hysteria and fear. If he fails to persuade the Klingons of his bona fides *he can expect to be treated with extreme prejudice. These are not hostage takers.*

The entire undertaking is misconceived. The locally settled Klingon population is not the central problem. Even should we succeed, such intelligence as can be gleaned about more important principals back home will no doubt be of dubious accuracy and limited value.

We should advise Star Fleet Headquarters to engage urgently with the grievances and aspirations of the Klingon people. Unless these are dealt with fair and square there cannot be a lasting peace.

The reply from JTK:

Your closeness to the relevant individual excuses what is otherwise an explosively communalist document. It is not for you to define the national interest nor to determine what undercover operations are to be undertaken. It is for you to enable such operations to occur and to provide back-up as and when required to do so. As a personal favour to you and in the name of my long friendship with your eminent Papaji I have destroyed your last without keeping a copy and suggest you do the same. Also destroy this.

Chekov asked Zulu to drive him up to Stratford for a performance of *Coriolanus*.

'How many kiddiwinks by now? Three?'

'Four,' said Zulu. 'All boys.'

'By the grace of God. She must be a good woman.'

'I have a full heart,' said Zulu, with sudden feeling. 'A full house, a full belly, a full bed.'

'Lucky so and so,' said Chekov. 'Always were warm-blooded. I, by contrast, am not. Reptiles, certain species of dinosaur, and me. I am in the wife market, by the way, if you know any suitable candidates. Bachelordom being, after a certain point, an obstacle on the career path.'

Zulu was driving strangely. In the slow lane of the motorway, as they approached an exit lane, he accelerated towards a hundred miles an hour. Once the exit was behind them, he slowed. Chekov noticed that he varied his speed and lane constantly. 'Doesn't the old rattletrap have cruise control?' he asked. 'Because, sport, this kind of performance would not do on the bridge of the flagship of the United Federation of Planets.'

'Anti-surveillance,' said Zulu. 'Dry-cleaning.' Chekov, alarmed, looked out of the back window.

'Have we been rumbled, then?'

'Nothing to worry about,' grinned Zulu. 'Better safe than sorry is all. Always anticipate the worst-case scenario.'

Chekov settled back in his seat. 'You liked toys and games,' he said. Zulu had been a crack rifle shot, the school's champion wrestler, and an expert fencer. 'Every Speech Day,' Zulu said, 'I would sit in the hall and clap, while you went up for all the work prizes. English Prize, History Prize, Latin Prize, Form Prize. Clap, clap, clap, term after term, year after year. But on Sports Day I got my cups. And now also I have my area of expertise.'

'Quite a reputation you're building up, if what I hear is anything to go by.'

There was a silence. England passed by at speed.

'Do you like Tolkien?' Zulu asked.

'I wouldn't have put you down as a big reader,' said Chekov, startled. 'No offence.'

'J.R.R. Tolkien,' said Zulu. '*The Lord of the Rings*.'

'Can't say I've read the gentleman. Heard of him, of course. Elves and pixies. Not your sort of thing at all, I'd have thought.'

'It is about a war to the finish between Good and Evil,' said Zulu intently. 'And while this great war is being fought there is one part of the world, the Shire, in which nobody even knows it's going on. The hobbits who live there work and squabble and make merry and they have no fucking clue about the forces that threaten them, and those that save their tiny skins.' His face was red with vehemence.

'Meaning me, I suppose,' Chekov said.

'I am a soldier in that war,' said Zulu. 'If you sit in an office you don't have one small idea of what the real world is like. The world of action, ji. The world of deeds, of things that are done and maybe undone too. The world of life and death.'

'Only in the worst case,' Chekov demurred.

'Do I tell you how to apply your smooth-tongued musca-polish to people's behinds?' stormed Zulu. 'Then do not tell me how to ply my trade.'

Soldiers going into battle pump themselves up, Chekov knew. This chest-beating was to be expected, it must not be misunderstood. 'When will you vamoose?' he quietly asked.

'Chekov ji, you won't see me go.'

Stratford approached. 'Did you know, ji,' Zulu offered, 'that the map of Tolkien's Middle-earth fits quite well over central England and Wales? Maybe all fairylands are right here, in our midst.'

'You're a deep one, old Zools,' said Chekov. 'Full of revelations today.'

Chekov had a few people over for dinner at his modern-style official residence in a private road in Hampstead: a Very Big Businessman he was wooing, journalists he liked, prominent India-lovers, noted Non-Resident Indians. The policy was business as usual. The dreadful event must not be seen to have derailed the ship of State: whose new captain, Chekov mused, was a former pilot himself. As if a Sulu, a Chekov had been suddenly promoted to the skipper's seat.

Damned difficult doing all this without a lady wife to act as hostess, he grumbled inwardly. The best golden plates with the many-headed lion at the centre, the finest crystal, the menu, the wines. Personnel had been seconded from India House to help him out, but it wasn't the same. The secrets of good evenings, like God, were in the details. Chekov meddled and fretted.

The evening went off well. Over brandy, Chekov even dared to introduce a blacker note. 'England has always been a breeding ground for our revolutionists,' he said. 'What would Pandit Nehru have been without Harrow? Or Gandhiji without his formative experiences here? Even the Pakistan idea was dreamt up by young radicals at college in what we then were asked to think of as the Mother Country. Now that England's status has declined, I suppose it is logical that the quality of the revolutionists she breeds has likewise fallen. The Kashmiris! Not a hope in hell. And as for these Khalistan types, let them not think that their evil deed has brought their dream a day closer. On the contrary. On the contrary. We will root them out and smash them to – what's the right word? – to *smithereens*.'

To his surprise he had begun speaking loudly and had risen to his feet. He sat down hard and laughed. The moment passed.

'The funny thing about this blasted nickname of mine', he said quickly to his dinner-table neighbour, the septuagenarian Very Big Businessman's improbably

ger seat inclined his head. 'Better
id. 'Don't tempt fate.'

through Middle-earth.

ey came off the motorway, Zulu
uit.'

he car. The two towers of Wembley
through a gap in the houses to the

those extremists manage to turn

be a fool. Who needs extremists
illings in Delhi? Hundreds, maybe
scalped and burned alive in front
–children, too.'

know who was behind it.'
red of evidence,' Chekov repeated

esses and photographs,' said Zulu.

who think', said Chekov slowly,
e Sikhs deserved what they got.'

ter than that, I hope,' said Chekov.
e, come on. All our bleddy lives.'
orkers have been indicted,' said

---

young and attractive wife, 'is that back then we never saw one episode of the TV series. No TV to see it on, you see. The whole thing was just a legend wafting its way from the US and UK to our lovely hill-station of Dehra Dun.

'After a while we got a couple of cheap paperback novelisations and passed them round as if they were naughty books like *Lady C* or some such. Lots of us tried the names on for size but only two of them stuck; probably because they seemed to go together, and the two of us got on pretty well, even though he was younger. A lovely boy. So just like Laurel and Hardy we were Chekov and Zulu.'

'Love and marriage,' said the woman.

'Beg pardon?'

'*You* know,' she said. 'Go together like is it milk and porridge. Or a car and garage, that's right. I love old songs. La-la-la-something-brother, you can't have fun without I think it's your mother.'

'Yes, now I do recall,' said Chekov.

3

Three months later Zulu telephoned his wife.

'O my God where have you vanished are you dead?'

'Listen please my bivi. Listen carefully my wife, my only love.'

'Yes. OK. I am calm. Line is bad, but.'

'Call Chekov and say condition red.'

'Arré! What is wrong with your condition?'

'Please. Condition red.'

'Yes. OK. Red.'

'Say the Klingons may be smelling things.'

'Clingers-on may be smelly things. Means what?'

'My darling, I beg you.'

'I have it all right here only. With this pencil I have written it, both.'

'Tell him, get Scotty to lock on to my signal and beam me up at once.'

'What rubbish! Even now you can't leave off that stupid game.'

'Bivi. It is urgent. *Beam me up.*'

Chekov dropped everything and drove. He went via the dry-cleaners as instructed; he drove round roundabouts twice, jumped red lights, deliberately took a wrong turning, stopped and turned round, made as many right turns as possible to see if anything followed him across the stream of traffic, and, on the motorway, mimicked Zulu's techniques. When he was as certain as he could be that he was clean, he headed for the rendezvous

Zulu. 'In spite of all the evidence of complicity. There-fore, I resign. You should quit, too.'

'If you have gone so damn radical,' cried Chekov, 'why hand over these lists at all? Why go only half the bleddy hog?'

'I am a security wallah,' said Zulu, opening the car door. 'Terrorists of all sorts are my foes. But not, appar-ently, in certain circumstances, yours.'

'Zulu, get in, damn it,' Chekov shouted. 'Don't you care for your career? A wife and four kiddiwinks to support. What about your old chums? Are you going to turn your back on me?'

But Zulu was already too far away.

Chekov and Zulu never met again. Zulu settled in Bombay and as the demand for private-sector protec-tion increased in that cash-rich boom-town, so his Zulu Shield and Zulu Spear companies prospered and grew. He had three more children, all of them boys, and remains happily married to this day.

As for Chekov, he never did take a wife. In spite of this supposed handicap, however, he did well in his chosen profession. His rapid rise continued. But one day in May 1991 he was, by chance, a member of the entourage accompanying Mr Rajiv Gandhi to the South Indian village of Sriperumbudur, where Rajiv was to address an election rally. Security was lax, intentionally so. In the previous election, Rajivji felt, the demands of security had placed an alienating barrier between himself and the electorate. On this occasion, he decreed, the voters must be allowed to feel close.

After the speeches, the Rajiv group descended from the podium. Chekov, who was just a few feet behind Rajiv, saw a small Tamil woman come forward, smiling. She shook Rajiv's hand and did not let go. Chekov understood what she was smiling about, and the knowledge was so powerful that it stopped time itself.

Because time had stopped, Chekov was able to make a number of private observations. 'These Tamil revolutionists are not England-returned,' he noted. 'So, finally, we have learned to produce the goods at home, and no longer need to import. Bang goes that old dinner-party standby; so to speak.' And, less dryly: 'The tragedy is not how one dies,' he thought. 'It is how one has lived.'

The scene around him vanished, dissolving in a pool of light, and was replaced by the bridge of the Starship *Enterprise*. All the leading figures were in their appointed places. Zulu sat beside Chekov at the front.

'Shields no longer operative,' Zulu was saying. On

So: thanks to her unexpected, somehow stomach-churning magic, he was no longer porter, but courter. 'Courter,' he repeated to the mirror when she had gone. His breath made a little dwindling picture of the word on the glass. 'Courter courter caught.' Okay. People called him many things, he did not mind. But this name, this courter, this he would try to be.

2

For years now I've been meaning to write down the story of Certainly-Mary, our ayah, the woman who did as much as my mother to raise my sisters and me, and her great adventure with her 'courter' in London, where we all lived for a time in the early Sixties in a block called Waverley House; but what with one thing and another I never got round to it.

Then recently I heard from Certainly-Mary after a longish silence. She wrote to say that she was ninety-one, had had a serious operation, and would I kindly send her some money, because she was embarrassed that her niece, with whom she was now living in the Kurla district of Bombay, was so badly out of pocket.

I sent the money, and soon afterwards received a pleasant letter from the niece, Stella, written in the same hand as the letter from 'Aya' – as we had always called Mary, palindromically dropping the 'h'. Aya had been so touched, the niece wrote, that I remembered her after all these years. 'I have been hearing the stories about you folks all my life,' the letter went on, 'and I think of you a little bit as family. Maybe you recall my mother, Mary's sister. She unfortunately passed on. Now it is I who write Mary's letters for her. We all wish you the best.'

This message from an intimate stranger reached out to me in my enforced exile from the beloved country of my birth and moved me, stirring things that had been buried very deep. Of course it also made me feel guilty about having done so little for Mary over the years. For whatever reason, it has become more important than ever to set down the story I've been carrying around unwritten for so long, the story of Aya and the gentle man whom she renamed – with unintentional but prophetic overtones of romance – 'the courter'. I see now that it is not just their story, but ours, mine, as well.

3

His real name was Mecir: you were supposed to say Mishirsh because it had invisible accents on it in some

Iron Curtain language in which the accents had to be invisible, my sister Durré said solemnly, in case somebody spied on them or rubbed them out or something. His first name also began with an m but it was so full of what we called Communist consonants, all those z's and c's and w's walled up together without vowels to give them breathing space, that I never even tried to learn it.

At first we thought of nicknaming him after a mischievous little comic-book character, Mr Mxyztplk from the Fifth Dimension, who looked a bit like Elmer Fudd and used to make Superman's life hell until ole Supe could trick him into saying his name backwards, Klptzyxm, whereupon he disappeared back into the Fifth Dimension; but because we weren't too sure how to say Mxyztplk (not to mention Klptzyxm) we dropped that idea. 'We'll just call you Mixed-Up,' I told him in the end, to simplify life. 'Mishter Mikshed-Up Mishirsh.' I was fifteen then and bursting with unemployed cock and it meant I could say things like that right into people's faces, even people less accommodating than Mr Mecir with his stroke.

What I remember most vividly are his pink rubber washing-up gloves, which he seemed never to remove, at least not until he came calling for Certainly-Mary . . .

At any rate, when I insulted him, with my sisters Durré and Muneeza cackling in the lift, Mecir just grinned an empty good-natured grin, nodded, 'You call me what you like, okay,' and went back to buffing and polishing the brasswork. There was no point teasing him if he was going to be like that, so I got into the lift and all the way to the fourth floor we sang *I Can't Stop Loving You* at the top of our best Ray Charles voices, which were pretty awful. But we were wearing our dark glasses, so it didn't matter.

4

It was the summer of 1962, and school was out. My baby sister Scheherazade was just one year old. Durré was a beehived fourteen; Muneeza was ten, and already quite a handful. The three of us – or rather Durré and me, with Muneeza trying desperately and unsuccessfully to be included in our gang – would stand over Scheherazade's cot and sing to her. 'No nursery rhymes,' Durré had decreed, and so there were none, for though she was a year my junior she was a natural leader. The infant Scheherazade's lullabies were our cover versions of recent hits by Chubby Checker, Neil Sedaka, Elvis and Pat Boone.

'Why don't you come home, Speedy Gonzales?' we bellowed in sweet disharmony: but most of all, and with actions, we would jump down, turn around and pick a bale of cotton. We would have jumped down, turned around and picked those bales all day except that the Maharaja of B— in the flat below complained, and Aya Mary came in to plead with us to be quiet.

'Look, see, it's Jumble-Aya who's fallen for Mixed-Up,' Durré shouted, and Mary blushed a truly immense blush. So naturally we segued right into a quick me-oh-my-oh; son of a gun, we had big fun. But then the baby began to yell, my father came in with his head down bull-fashion and steaming from both ears, and we needed all the good luck charms we could find.

I had been at boarding school in England for a year or so when Abba took the decision to bring the family over. Like all his decisions, it was neither explained to nor discussed with anyone, not even my mother. When they first arrived he rented two adjacent flats in a seedy Bayswater mansion block called Graham Court, which lurked furtively in a nothing street that crawled along the side of the ABC Queensway cinema towards the Porchester Baths. He commandeered one of these flats for himself and put my mother, three sisters and Aya in the other; also, on school holidays, me. England, where liquor was freely available, did little for my father's *bonhomie*, so in a way it was a relief to have a flat to ourselves.

Most nights he emptied a bottle of Johnnie Walker Red Label and a soda-siphon. My mother did not dare to go across to 'his place' in the evenings. She said: 'He makes faces at me.'

Aya Mary took Abba his dinner and answered all his calls (if he wanted anything, he would phone us up and ask for it). I am not sure why Mary was spared his drunken rages. She said it was because she was nine years his senior, so she could tell him to show due respect.

After a few months, however, my father leased a three-bedroom fourth-floor apartment with a fancy address. This was Waverley House in Kensington Court, W8. Among its other residents were not one but two Indian Maharajas, the sporting Prince P— as well as the old B— who has already been mentioned. Now we were jammed in together, my parents and Baby Scare-zade (as her siblings had affectionately begun to call her) in the master bedroom, the three of us in a much smaller room, and Mary, I regret to admit, on a straw mat laid on the fitted carpet in the hall. The third bedroom became my father's office, where he made phone-calls and kept his *Encyclopaedia Britannica*, his *Reader's Digest*s, and (under lock and key) the television cabinet. We entered it at our peril. It was the Minotaur's lair.

One morning he was persuaded to drop in at the corner pharmacy and pick up some supplies for the baby. When he returned there was a hurt, schoolboyish look on his face that I had never seen before, and he was pressing his hand against his cheek.

'She hit me,' he said plaintively.

'Hai! Allah-tobah! Darling!' cried my mother, fussing. 'Who hit you? Are you injured? Show me, let me see.'

'I did nothing,' he said, standing there in the hall with the pharmacy bag in his other hand and a face as pink as Mecir's rubber gloves. 'I just went in with your list. The girl seemed very helpful. I asked for baby compound, Johnson's powder, teething jelly, and she brought them out. Then I asked did she have any nipples, and she slapped my face.'

My mother was appalled. 'Just for that?' And Certainly-Mary backed her up. 'What is this nonsense?' she wanted to know. 'I have been in that chemist's shock, and they have flenty nickels, different sizes, all on view.'

Durré and Muneeza could not contain themselves. They were rolling round on the floor, laughing and kicking their legs in the air.

'You both shut your face at once,' my mother ordered. 'A madwoman has hit your father. Where is the comedy?'

'I don't believe it,' Durré gasped. 'You just went up to that girl and said,' and here she fell apart again, stamping her feet and holding her stomach, ' *"have you got any nipples?"* '

My father grew thunderous, empurpled. Durré controlled herself. 'But Abba,' she said, at length, 'here they call them teats.'

Now my mother's and Mary's hands flew to their mouths, and even my father looked shocked. 'But how shameless!' my mother said. 'The same word as for what's on your bosoms?' She coloured, and stuck out her tongue for shame.

'These English,' sighed Certainly-Mary. 'But aren't they the limit? Certainly-yes; they are.'

I remember this story with delight, because it was the only time I ever saw my father so discomfited, and the incident became legendary and the girl in the pharmacy was installed as the object of our great veneration. (Durré and I went in there just to take a look at her –

she was a plain, short girl of about seventeen, with large, unavoidable breasts – but she caught us whispering and glared so fiercely that we fled.) And also because in the general hilarity I was able to conceal the shaming truth that I, who had been in England for so long, would have made the same mistake as Abba did.

It wasn't just Certainly-Mary and my parents who had trouble with the English language. My schoolfellows tittered when in my Bombay way I said 'brought-up' for upbringing (as in 'where was your brought-up?') and 'thrice' for three times and 'quarter-plate' for side-plate and 'macaroni' for pasta in general. As for learning the difference between nipples and teats, I really hadn't had any opportunities to increase my word power in that area at all.

5

So I was a little jealous of Certainly-Mary when Mixed-Up came to call. He rang our bell, his body quivering with deference in an old suit grown too loose, the trousers tightly gathered by a belt; he had taken off his rubber gloves and there were roses in his hand. My father opened the door and gave him a withering look. Being a snob, Abba was not pleased that the flat lacked a separate service entrance, so that even a porter had to be treated as a member of the same universe as himself.

'Mary,' Mixed-Up managed, licking his lips and pushing back his floppy white hair. 'I, to see Miss Mary, come, am.'

'Wait on,' Abba said, and shut the door in his face.

Certainly-Mary spent all her afternoons off with old Mixed-Up from then on, even though that first date was not a complete success. He took her 'up West' to show her the visitors' London she had never seen, but at the top of an up escalator at Piccadilly Circus, while Mecir was painfully enunciating the words on the posters she couldn't read – *Unzip a banana*, and *Idris when I's dri* – she got her sari stuck in the jaws of the machine, and as the escalator pulled at the garment it began to unwind. She was forced to spin round and round like a top, and screamed at the top of her voice, 'O BAAP! BAAPU–RÉ! BAAP–RÉ–BAAP–RÉ–BAAP!' It was Mixed-Up who saved her by pushing the emergency stop button before the sari was completely unwound and she was exposed in her petticoat for all the world to see.

'O, courter!' she wept on his shoulder. 'O, no more escaleater, courter, nevermore, surely not!'

———

My own amorous longings were aimed at Durré's best friend, a Polish girl called Rozalia, who had a holiday job at Faiman's shoe shop on Oxford Street. I pursued her pathetically throughout the holidays and, on and off, for the next two years. She would let me have lunch with her sometimes and buy her a Coke and a sandwich, and once she came with me to stand on the terraces at White Hart Lane to watch Jimmy Greaves's first game for the Spurs. 'Come on you whoi-oites,' we both shouted dutifully. 'Come on you *Lily-whoites*.' After that she even invited me into the back room at Faiman's, where she kissed me twice and let me touch her breast, but that was as far as I got.

And then there was my sort-of-cousin Chandni, whose mother's sister had married my mother's brother, though they had since split up. Chandni was eighteen months older than me, and so sexy it made you sick. She was training to be an Indian classical dancer, Odissi as well as Natyam, but in the meantime she dressed in tight black jeans and a clinging black polo-neck jumper and took me, now and then, to hang out at Bunjie's, where she knew most of the folk-music crowd that frequented the place, and where she answered to the name of Moonlight, which is what *chandni* means. I chain-smoked with the folkies and then went to the toilet to throw up.

Chandni was the stuff of obsessions. She was a teen-age dream, the Moon River come to Earth like the Goddess Ganga, dolled up in slinky black. But for her I was just the young greenhorn cousin to whom she was being nice because he hadn't learned his way around.

She-E-rry, won't you come out tonight? yodelled the Four Seasons. I knew exactly how they felt. *Come, come, come out toni-yi-yight.* And while you're at it, love me do.

6

They went for walks in Kensington Gardens. 'Pan,' Mixed-Up said, pointing at a statue. 'Los' boy. Nev' grew up.' They went to Barkers and Pontings and Derry & Toms and picked out furniture and curtains for imaginary homes. They cruised supermarkets and chose little delicacies to eat. In Mecir's cramped lounge they sipped what he called 'chimpanzee tea' and toasted crumpets in front of an electric bar fire.

Thanks to Mixed-Up, Mary was at last able to watch television. She liked children's programmes best, especially *The Flintstones*. Once, giggling at her daring, Mary confided to Mixed-Up that Fred and Wilma reminded her of her Sahib and Begum Sahiba upstairs; at which the courter, matching her audaciousness, pointed first at Certainly-Mary and then at himself, grinned a wide gappy smile and said, 'Rubble.'

Later, on the news, a vulpine Englishman with a thin moustache and mad eyes declaimed a warning about immigrants, and Certainly-Mary flapped her hand at the set: 'Khali-pili bom marta,' she objected, and then, for her host's benefit translated: 'For nothing he is shouting shouting. Bad life! Switch it off.'

They were often interrupted by the Maharajas of B— and P—, who came downstairs to escape their wives and ring other women from the call-box in the porter's room.

'Oh, baby, forget that guy,' said sporty Prince P—, who seemed to spend all his days in tennis whites, and whose plump gold Rolex was almost lost in the thick hair on his arm. 'I'll show you a better time than him, baby; step into my world.'

The Maharaja of B— was older, uglier, more matter-of-fact. 'Yes, bring all appliances. Room is booked in name of Mr Douglas Home. Six forty-five to seven fifteen. You have printed rate card? Please. Also a two-foot ruler, must be wooden. Frilly apron, plus.'

This is what has lasted in my memory of Waverley House, this seething mass of bad marriages, booze, philanderers and unfulfilled young lusts; of the Maharaja of P— roaring away towards London's casinoland every night, in a red sports car with fitted blondes, and of the Maharaja of B— skulking off to Kensington High Street wearing dark glasses in the dark, and a coat with the collar turned up even though it was high summer; and at the heart of our little universe were Certainly-Mary and her courter, drinking chimpanzee tea and singing along with the national anthem of Bedrock.

But they were not really like Barney and Betty Rubble at all. They were formal, polite. They were . . . courtly. He courted her, and, like a coy, ringleted ingénue with a fan, she inclined her head, and entertained his suit.

7

I spent one half-term weekend in 1963 at the home in Beccles, Suffolk of Field Marshal Sir Charles Lutwidge-Dodgson, an old India hand and a family friend who was supporting my application for British citizenship. 'The Dodo', as he was known, invited me down by myself, saying he wanted to get to know me better.

He was a huge man whose skin had started hanging too loosely on his face, a giant living in a tiny thatched cottage and forever bumping his head. No wonder he was irascible at times; he was in Hell, a Gulliver trapped in that rose-garden Lilliput of croquet hoops, church bells, sepia photographs and old battle-trumpets.

The weekend was fitful and awkward until the Dodo asked if I played chess. Slightly awestruck at the prospect of playing a Field Marshal, I nodded; and ninety minutes later, to my amazement, won the game.

I went into the kitchen, strutting somewhat, planning to boast a little to the old soldier's long-time house-keeper, Mrs Liddell. But as soon as I entered she said: 'Don't tell me. You never went and won?'

'Yes,' I said, affecting nonchalance. 'As a matter of fact, yes, I did.'

'Gawd,' said Mrs Liddell. 'Now there'll be hell to

pay. You go back in there and ask him for another game, and this time make sure you lose.'

I did as I was told, but was never invited to Beccles again.

Still, the defeat of the Dodo gave me new confidence at the chessboard, so when I returned to Waverley House after finishing my O levels, and was at once invited to play a game by Mixed-Up (Mary had told him about my victory in the Battle of Beccles with great pride and some hyperbole), I said: 'Sure, I don't mind.' How long could it take to thrash the old duffer, after all?

There followed a massacre royal. Mixed-Up did not just beat me; he had me for breakfast, over easy. I couldn't believe it – the canny opening, the fluency of his combination play, the force of his attacks, my own impossibly cramped, strangled positions – and asked for a second game. This time he tucked into me even more heartily. I sat broken in my chair at the end, close to tears. *Big girls don't cry*, I reminded myself, but the song went on playing in my head: *That's just an alibi*.

'Who are you?' I demanded, humiliation weighing down every syllable. 'The devil in disguise?'

Mixed-Up gave his big, silly grin. 'Grand Master,' he said. 'Long time. Before head.'

———

'You're a Grand Master,' I repeated, still in a daze. Then in a moment of horror I remembered that I had seen the name Mecir in books of classic games. 'Nimzo-Indian,' I said aloud. He beamed and nodded furiously.

'That Mecir?' I asked wonderingly.

'That,' he said. There was saliva dribbling out of a corner of his sloppy old mouth. This ruined old man was in the books. He was in the books. And even with his mind turned to rubble he could still wipe the floor with me.

'Now play lady,' he grinned. I didn't get it. 'Mary lady,' he said. 'Yes yes certainly.'

She was pouring tea, waiting for my answer. 'Aya, you can't play,' I said, bewildered.

'Learning, baba,' she said. 'What is it, na? Only a game.'

And then she, too, beat me senseless, and with the black pieces, at that. It was not the greatest day of my life.

8

From *100 Most Instructive Chess Games* by Robert Reshevsky, 1961:

M. Mecir – M. Najdorf
Dallas 1950, Nimzo-Indian Defense

The attack of a tactician can be troublesome to meet – that of a strategist even more so. Whereas the tactician's threats may be unmistakable, the strategist confuses the issue by keeping things in abeyance. He threatens to threaten!

Take this game for instance: Mecir posts a Knight at Q6 to get a grip on the center. Then he establishes a passed Pawn on one wing to occupy his opponent on the Queen side. Finally he stirs up the position on the Kingside. What does the poor bewildered opponent do? How can he defend everything at once? Where will the blow fall?

Watch Mecir keep Najdorf on the run, as he shifts the attack from side to side!

Chess had become their private language. Old Mixed-Up, lost as he was for words, retained, on the chessboard, much of the articulacy and subtlety which had vanished from his speech. As Certainly-Mary gained in skill – and she had learned with astonishing speed, I thought bitterly, for someone who couldn't read or write or pronounce the letter p – she was better able to understand, and respond to, the wit of the reduced maestro with whom she had so unexpectedly forged a bond.

He taught her with great patience, showing-not-telling, repeating openings and combinations and endgame techniques over and over until she began to see the meaning in the patterns. When they played, he handicapped himself, he told her her best moves and demonstrated their consequences, drawing her, step by step, into the infinite possibilities of the game.

Such was their courtship. 'It is like an adventure, baba,' Mary once tried to explain to me. 'It is like going with him to his country, you know? What a place, baap-ré! Beautiful and dangerous and funny and full of fuzzles. For me it is a big-big discovery. What to tell you? I go for the game. It is a wonder.'

I understood, then, how far things had gone between them. Certainly-Mary had never married, and had made it clear to old Mixed-Up that it was too late to start any of that monkey business at her age. The courter was a widower, and had grown-up children somewhere, lost long ago behind the ever-higher walls of Eastern Europe. But in the game of chess they had found a form of flirtation, an endless renewal that precluded the possibility of boredom, a courtly wonderland of the ageing heart.

What would the Dodo have made of it all? No doubt it would have scandalised him to see chess, chess of all games, the great formalisation of war, transformed into an art of love.

As for me: my defeats by Certainly-Mary and her courter ushered in further humiliations. Durré and Muneeza went down with the mumps, and so, finally, in spite of my mother's efforts to segregate us, did I. I lay terrified in bed while the doctor warned me not to stand up and move around if I could possibly help it. 'If you do,' he said, 'your parents won't need to punish you. You will have punished yourself quite enough.'

I spent the following few weeks tormented day and night by visions of grotesquely swollen testicles and a subsequent life of limp impotence – finished before I'd even started, it wasn't fair! – which were made much worse by my sisters' quick recovery and incessant gibes. But in the end I was lucky; the illness didn't spread to the deep South. 'Think how happy your hundred and one girlfriends will be, bhai,' sneered Durré, who knew all about my continued failures in the Rozalia and Chandni departments.

On the radio, people were always singing about the joys of being sixteen years old. I wondered where they were, all those boys and girls of my age having the time of their lives. Were they driving around America in Studebaker convertibles? They certainly weren't in my neighbourhood. London, W8 was Sam Cooke country that summer. *Another Saturday night* . . . There might be a mop-top love-song stuck at number one, but I was down with lonely Sam in the lower depths of the charts, how-I-wishing I had someone, etc., and generally feeling in a pretty goddamn dreadful way.

9

'Baba, come quick.'

It was late at night when Aya Mary shook me awake. After many urgent hisses, she managed to drag me out of sleep and pull me, pajama'ed and yawning, down the hall. On the landing outside our flat was Mixed-Up the courter, huddled up against a wall, weeping. He had a black eye and there was dried blood on his mouth.

'What happened?' I asked Mary, shocked.

'Men,' wailed Mixed-Up. 'Threaten. Beat.'

He had been in his lounge earlier that evening when the sporting Maharaja of P— burst in to say, 'If anybody comes looking for me, okay, any tough-guy type guys, okay, I am out, okay? Oh you tea. Don't let them go upstairs, okay? Big tip, okay?'

A short time later, the old Maharaja of B— also arrived in Mecir's lounge, looking distressed.

'Suno, listen on,' said the Maharaja of B—. 'You don't know where I am, samajh liya? Understood? Some low persons may inquire. You don't know. I am abroad, achha? On extended travels abroad. Do your job, porter. Handsome recompense.'

Late at night two tough-guy types did indeed turn up. It seemed the hairy Prince P— had gambling debts. 'Out,' Mixed-Up grinned in his sweetest way. The tough-guy types nodded, slowly. They had long hair and thick lips like Mick Jagger's. 'He's a busy gent. We should of made an appointment,' said the first type to the second. 'Didn't I tell you we should of called?'

'You did,' agreed the second type. 'Got to do these things right, you said, he's royalty. And you was right, my son, I put my hand up, I was dead wrong. I put my hand up to that.'

'Let's leave our card,' said the first type. 'Then he'll know to expect us.'

'Ideal,' said the second type, and smashed his fist into old Mixed-Up's mouth. 'You tell him,' the second type said, and struck the old man in the eye. 'When he's in. You mention it.'

He had locked the front door after that; but much later, well after midnight, there was a hammering.

Mixed-Up called out, 'Who?'

'We are close friends of the Maharaja of B—' said a voice. 'No, I tell a lie. Acquaintances.'

'He calls upon a lady of our acquaintance,' said a second voice. 'To be precise.'

'It is in that connection that we crave audience,' said the first voice.

'Gone,' said Mecir. 'Jet plane. Gone.'

There was a silence. Then the second voice said, 'Can't be in the jet set if you never jump on a jet, eh? Biarritz, Monte, all of that.'

'Be sure and let His Highness know', said the first voice, 'that we eagerly await his return.'

'With regard to our mutual friend,' said the second voice. 'Eagerly.'

What does the poor bewildered opponent do? The words from the chess book popped unbidden into my head. *How can he defend everything at once? Where will the blow fall? Watch Mecir keep Najdorf on the run, as he shifts the attack from side to side!*

Mixed-Up returned to his lounge and on this occasion, even though there had been no use of force, he began to weep. After a time he took the elevator up to the fourth floor and whispered through our letter-box to Certainly-Mary sleeping on her mat.

'I didn't want to wake Sahib,' Mary said. 'You know his trouble, na? And Begum Sahiba is so tired at end of the day. So now you tell, baba, what to do?'

What did she expect me to come up with? I was sixteen years old. 'Mixed-Up must call the police,' I unoriginally offered.

'No, no, baba,' said Certainly-Mary emphatically. 'If the courter makes a scandal for Maharaja-log, then in the end it is the courter only who will be out on his ear.'

I had no other ideas. I stood before them feeling like a fool, while they both turned upon me their frightened, supplicant eyes.

'Go to sleep,' I said. 'We'll think about it in the morning.' *The first pair of thugs were tacticians*, I was thinking. *They were troublesome to meet. But the second pair were scarier; they were strategists. They threatened to threaten.*

Nothing happened in the morning, and the sky was clear. It was almost impossible to believe in fists, and menacing voices at the door. During the course of the day both Maharajas visited the porter's lounge and stuck five-pound notes in Mixed-Up's waistcoat pocket. 'Held the fort, good man,' said Prince P—, and the Maharaja of B— echoed those sentiments: 'Spot on. All handled now, achha? Problem over.'

The three of us – Aya Mary, her courter, and me – held a council of war that afternoon and decided that no further action was necessary. The hall porter was the front line in any such situation, I argued, and the front line had held. And now the risks were past. Assurances had been given. End of story.

'End of story,' repeated Certainly-Mary doubtfully, but then, seeking to reassure Mecir, she brightened. 'Correct,' she said. 'Most certainly! All-done, finis.' She slapped her hands against each other for emphasis. She asked Mixed-Up if he wanted a game of chess; but for once the courter didn't want to play.

10

After that I was distracted, for a time, from the story of Mixed-Up and Certainly-Mary by violence nearer home.

My middle sister Muneeza, now eleven, was entering her delinquent phase a little early. She was the true inheritor of my father's black rage, and when she lost control it was terrible to behold. That summer she seemed to pick fights with my father on purpose; seemed prepared, at her young age, to test her strength against his. (I intervened in her rows with Abba only once, in the kitchen. She grabbed the kitchen scissors and flung them at me. They cut me on the thigh. After that I kept my distance.)

As I witnessed their wars I felt myself coming unstuck from the idea of family itself. I looked at my screaming sister and thought how brilliantly self-destructive she was, how triumphantly she was ruining her relations with the people she needed most.

And I looked at my choleric, face-pulling father and thought about British citizenship. My existing Indian passport permitted me to travel only to a very few countries, which were carefully listed on the second right-hand page. But I might soon have a British passport and then, by hook or by crook, I would get away from him. I would not have this face-pulling in my life.

At sixteen, you still think you can escape from your father. You aren't listening to his voice speaking through your mouth, you don't see how your gestures already mirror his; you don't see him in the way you hold your body, in the way you sign your name. You don't hear his whisper in your blood.

On the day I have to tell you about, my two-year-old sister Chhoti Scheherazade, Little Scare-zade, started crying as she often did during one of our family rows. Amma and Aya Mary loaded her into her push-chair

and made a rapid getaway. They pushed her to Kensington Square and then sat on the grass, turned Scheherazade loose and made philosophical remarks while she
tired herself out. Finally, she fell asleep, and they made
their way home in the fading light of the evening. Outside Waverley House they were approached by two
well-turned-out young men with Beatle haircuts and
the buttoned-up, collarless jackets made popular by the
band. The first of these young men asked my mother,
very politely, if she might be the Maharani of B—.

'No,' my mother answered, flattered.

'Oh, but you are, madam,' said the second Beatle,
equally politely. 'For you are heading for Waverley
House and that is the Maharaja's place of residence.'

'No, no,' my mother said, still blushing with
pleasure. 'We are a different Indian family.'

'Quite so,' the first Beatle nodded understandingly,
and then, to my mother's great surprise, placed a finger
alongside his nose, and winked. 'Incognito, eh. Mum's
the word.'

'Now excuse us,' my mother said, losing patience.
'We are not the ladies you seek.'

The second Beatle tapped a foot lightly against a
wheel of the push-chair. 'Your husband seeks ladies,
madam, were you aware of that fact? Yes, he does.
Most assiduously, may I add.'

'Too assiduously,' said the first Beatle, his face darkening.

'I tell you I am not the Maharani Begum,' my mother said, growing suddenly alarmed. 'Her business is not my business. Kindly let me pass.'

The second Beatle stepped closer to her. She could feel his breath, which was minty. 'One of the ladies he sought out was our ward, as you might say,' he explained. 'That would be the term. Under our protection, you follow. Us, therefore, being responsible for her welfare.'

'Your husband', said the first Beatle, showing his teeth in a frightening way, and raising his voice one notch, 'damaged the goods. Do you hear me, Queenie? He damaged the fucking goods.'

'Mistaken identity, fleas,' said Certainly-Mary. 'Many Indian residents in Waverley House. We are decent ladies; *fleas*.'

The second Beatle had taken out something from an inside pocket. A blade caught the light. 'Fucking wogs,' he said. 'You fucking come over here, you don't fucking know how to fucking behave. Why don't you fucking fuck off to fucking Wogistan? Fuck your fucking wog arses. Now then,' he added in a quiet voice, holding up the knife, 'unbutton your blouses.'

———

Just then a loud noise emanated from the doorway of
Waverley House. The two women and the two men
turned to look, and out came Mixed-Up, yelling at the
top of his voice and windmilling his arms like a mad
old loon.

'Hullo,' said the Beatle with the knife, looking
amused. 'Who's this, then? Oh oh fucking seven?'

Mixed-Up was trying to speak, he was in a mighty
agony of effort, but all that was coming out of his
mouth was raw, unshaped noise. Scheherazade woke
up and joined in. The two Beatles looked displeased.
But then something happened inside old Mixed-Up;
something popped, and in a great rush he gabbled,
'Sirs sirs no sirs these not B— women sirs B— women
upstairs on floor three sirs Maharaja of B— also sirs
God's truth mother's grave swear.'

It was the longest sentence he had spoken since the
stroke that had broken his tongue long ago.

And what with his torrent and Scheherazade's
squalls there were suddenly heads poking out from
doorways, attention was being paid, and the two
Beatles nodded gravely. 'Honest mistake,' the first of
them said apologetically to my mother, and actually
bowed from the waist. 'Could happen to anyone,' the
knife-man added, ruefully. They turned and began to
walk quickly away. As they passed Mecir, however, they

paused. 'I know you, though,' said the knife-man. ' "*Jet plane. Gone.*" ' He made a short movement of the arm, and then Mixed-Up the courter was lying on the pavement with blood leaking from a wound in his stomach. 'All okay now,' he gasped, and passed out.

I I

He was on the road to recovery by Christmas; my mother's letter to the landlords, in which she called him a 'knight in shining armour', ensured that he was well looked after, and his job was kept open for him. He continued to live in his little ground-floor cubby-hole, while the hall porter's duties were carried out by shift-duty staff. 'Nothing but the best for our very own hero,' the landlords assured my mother in their reply.

The two Maharajas and their retinues had moved out before I came home for the Christmas holidays, so we had no further visits from the Beatles or the Rolling Stones. Certainly-Mary spent as much time as she could with Mecir; but it was the look of my old Aya that worried me more than poor Mixed-Up. She looked older, and powdery, as if she might crumble away at any moment into dust.

'We didn't want to worry you at school,' my mother

said. 'She has been having heart trouble. Palpitations. Not all the time, but.'

Mary's health problems had sobered up the whole family. Muneeza's tantrums had stopped, and even my father was making an effort. They had put up a Christmas tree in the sitting-room and decorated it with all sorts of baubles. It was so odd to see a Christmas tree at our place that I realised things must be fairly serious.

On Christmas Eve my mother suggested that Mary might like it if we all sang some carols. Amma had made song-sheets, six copies, by hand. When we did *O come, all ye faithful* I showed off by singing from memory in Latin. Everybody behaved perfectly. When Muneeza suggested that we should try *Swinging on a Star* or *I Wanna Hold Your Hand* instead of this boring stuff, she wasn't really being serious. So this is family life, I thought. This is it.

But we were only play-acting.

A few weeks earlier, at school, I'd come across an American boy, the star of the school's Rugby football team, crying in the Chapel cloisters. I asked him what the matter was and he told me that President Kennedy had been assassinated. 'I don't believe you,' I said, but I could see that it was true. The football star sobbed and sobbed. I took his hand.

'When the President dies, the nation is orphaned,' he eventually said, broken-heartedly parroting a piece of cracker-barrel wisdom he'd probably heard on Voice of America.

'I know how you feel,' I lied. 'My father just died, too.'

Mary's heart trouble turned out to be a mystery; unpredictably, it came and went. She was subjected to all sorts of tests during the next six months, but each time the doctors ended up by shaking their heads: they couldn't find anything wrong with her. Physically, she was right as rain; except that there were these periods when her heart kicked and bucked in her chest like the wild horses in *The Misfits*, the ones whose roping and tying made Marilyn Monroe so mad.

Mecir went back to work in the spring, but his experience had knocked the stuffing out of him. He was slower to smile, duller of eye, more inward. Mary, too, had turned in upon herself. They still met for tea, crumpets and *The Flintstones*, but something was no longer quite right.

At the beginning of the summer Mary made an announcement.

'I know what is wrong with me,' she told my parents, out of the blue. 'I need to go home.'

'But, Aya,' my mother argued, 'homesickness is not a real disease.'

'God knows for what-all we came over to this country,' Mary said. 'But I can no longer stay. No. Certainly not.' Her determination was absolute.

So it was England that was breaking her heart, breaking it by not being India. London was killing her, by not being Bombay. And Mixed-Up? I wondered. Was the courter killing her, too, because he was no longer himself? Or was it that her heart, roped by two different loves, was being pulled both East and West, whinnying and rearing, like those movie horses being yanked this way by Clark Gable and that way by Montgomery Clift, and she knew that to live she would have to choose?

'I must go,' said Certainly-Mary. 'Yes, certainly. *Bas*. Enough.'

That summer, the summer of '64, I turned seventeen. Chandni went back to India. Durré's Polish friend Rozalia informed me over a sandwich in Oxford Street that she was getting engaged to a 'real man', so I could forget about seeing her again, because this Zbigniew was the jealous type. Roy Orbison sang *It's Over* in my ears as I walked away to the Tube, but the truth was that nothing had really begun.

Certainly-Mary left us in mid-July. My father bought her a one-way ticket to Bombay, and that last morning was heavy with the pain of ending. When we took her bags down to the car, Mecir the hall porter was nowhere to be seen. Mary did not knock on the door of his lounge, but walked straight out through the freshly polished oak-panelled lobby, whose mirrors and brasses were sparkling brightly; she climbed into the back seat of our Ford Zodiac and sat there stiffly with her carry-on grip on her lap, staring straight ahead. I had known and loved her all my life. *Never mind your damned courter*, I wanted to shout at her, *what about me?*

As it happened, she was right about the homesickness. After her return to Bombay, she never had a day's heart trouble again; and, as the letter from her niece Stella confirmed, at ninety-one she was still going strong.

Soon after she left, my father told us he had decided to 'shift location' to Pakistan. As usual, there were no discussions, no explanations, just the simple fiat. He gave up the lease on the flat in Waverley House at the end of the summer holidays, and they all went off to Karachi, while I went back to school.

I became a British citizen that year. I was one of the lucky ones, I guess, because in spite of that chess game

I had the Dodo on my side. And the passport did, in many ways, set me free. It allowed me to come and go, to make choices that were not the ones my father would have wished. But I, too, have ropes around my neck, I have them to this day, pulling me this way and that, East and West, the nooses tightening, commanding, *choose, choose*.

I buck, I snort, I whinny, I rear, I kick. Ropes, I do not choose between you. Lassoes, lariats, I choose neither of you, and both. Do you hear? I refuse to choose.

A year or so after we moved out I was in the area and dropped in at Waverley House to see how the old courter was doing. Maybe, I thought, we could have a game of chess, and he could beat me to a pulp. The lobby was empty, so I knocked on the door of his little lounge. A stranger answered.

'Where's Mixed-Up?' I cried, taken by surprise. I apologised at once, embarrassed. 'Mr Mecir, I meant, the porter.'

'I'm the porter, sir,' the man said. 'I don't know anything about any mix-up.'

ACKNOWLEDGMENTS

Six of these stories have been published previously, although in somewhat different form. They first appeared in the following places:

'Good Advice Is Rarer Than Rubies' in the *New Yorker*; 'The Free Radio' in *Atlantic Monthly*; 'The Prophet's Hair' in *London Review of Books*; 'Yorick" in *Encounter*; 'At the Auction of the Ruby Slippers' in *Granta*; and 'Christopher Columbus and Queen Isabella of Spain' in the *New Yorker*.

'The Harmony of the Spheres', 'Chekov and Zulu' and 'The Courter' have not been published before.

'The Harmony of the Spheres' relies, for some of its occultist material, on the writings of James Webb, especially *The Occult Underground* (Open Court, Illinois, 1974) and *The Harmonious Circle* (Putnam, 1980).

In 'The Courter', the author wishes to thank Ardmore & Beechwood Ltd, London WC2H0EA, for permission to reproduce 'Sherry' (words and music by Bob Gaudio) © 1962, Claridge Music Inc., USA.

The passage quoted on page 194 is in tact an account of a game between S. Reshevsky and M. Najdorf, played in 1957 and described in *The Most Instructive Games of Chess Ever Played*, by Irving Chernev (Faber and Faber, 1966).

Finally, thanks to Bill Buford, Susannah Clapp and Bob Gottlieb; Sonny Mehta and Erroll McDonald; and Frances Coady and Caroline Michel.